Thief by Night

Thief, Volume 1

Hari Sinclair

Published by Purple Nib Press, 2019.

Purple Nib
Press

DEDICATION

To Simon-Jay and Xander.
Not all cheerleaders carry pompoms.

ACKNOWLEDGMENTS

All the thanks to Chris, Lila and Jana for beta reading, editing and proofreading. Without your polishing, this story would still be in a drawer, still gathering dust.

~

Much love to my fellow Left to Write server members. Your support and encouragement got me through the roughest moments.

~

Thanks to my sounding board, Kerry. Your enthusiasm and endless patience mean the whole world to me.

PROLOGUE

The jewel was in the grasp of his gloved hand.

It had been easy. No flashing lights, no alarms, no security guards and no complicated locks to bypass. Not even a display case to break. All he needed was one security pass. All he had to do was pluck the diamond from its mount, put it in his pocket and saunter out through the front door.

It was too easy.

Most jobs were more complicated than this. He had to charm his way into a place, analyze the building's weak spots, take advantage of human error and choose his moment. He was an expert at this; he didn't make mistakes.

Until tonight.

Vibrations from the hallway reached the soles of his feet and his heart began pounding in his chest. He must have tripped the sensor of a silent alarm when he touched the gem.

Panic rose as the voices drew closer. Beeping sounds from the keypad behind the ancient wooden door told him they were close. It shouldn't be happening like this; he did everything right.

The naive young curator, Rose was a romantic at heart, so it was easy for him to woo her and lift her security pass; all it took was a charming smile and a laugh at the right jokes. She was so giddy with excitement that she enthusiastically offered to give him a tour of Prince Ahmed's private art collection. That gave him the chance to reconnoitre the gallery. He was, of course, invited to the unveiling party for Prince Ahmed's latest find, an

1893 Midnight Fabergé egg. While everyone's focus was on the egg, he was free to sneak out of the party and steal the 6 carat vivid pink Argyle diamond from the other side of the building. If all went to plan, he would have rejoined the party with the diamond in his pocket before the master of ceremonies announced the dessert table. He would make sure to slip the pass back into Rose's pocket before she noticed it was gone, then make sure he was seen mingling with the right people. He'd be home before anybody noticed something was amiss.

That was the plan.

Instead, he was trapped.

Suddenly, and from nowhere, a woman in black appeared in front of him. Inquisitive eyes darted over his face and her lips twitched into a smirk. Before an exclamation could leave his lungs, she pressed a finger to her lips, warning him to stay quiet. Wordlessly, she wound herself around him, holding him across his back, under his arms. He felt her weight shift as her legs snaked around his waist and her feet hooked behind his knees. She pressed her face into the crook of his neck.

"Hold on."

He had barely registered the shock at this new development when they lifted off the ground. He wrapped his arms around her for stability as his own feet left the floor. Her body stiffened and her hands gripped his jacket as they reached the rafters.

The guards entered the room, darting around the exhibits, checking behind and under every installation. Torch-light flashed across the floor and into corners of the room, lighting up paintings and artefacts. Nobody looked up.

"False alarm!" One called out.

"We need to get the geeks in to fix the system, it's still glitching," another said.

The guards retreated as quickly as they arrived.

He felt the woman exhale before they began to descend. They were a metre from the floor when she started to unwrap herself from his person, letting him drop the last thirty centimetres to the polished parquet. Seconds later, she landed lightly next to him.

White-blonde braided hair jutted from a black beanie hat above a black domino mask. She wore tight black jeans, combat boots and a black biker jacket with a silver zip running up the centre. She was almost monochrome. The only hints of colour were intense blue eyes that lingered on his face and pink lips that curled upwards like she had thought of a joke but wasn't willing to share it.

"Thank you," he said, barely audible.

"It's nothing," she said. Her voice was sultry, her accent neutral. Her face was centimetres from his. "Maybe you can repay the favour sometime? Something tells me our paths will cross again."

She kicked back as she triggered the rope mechanism, arching around a sturdy rafter in a perfectly timed movement, before swinging back to land with tiptoes on it. Without his added weight, she moved much faster, and she was retreating from the building before he realised it.

Before he noticed.

She had the diamond.

1

Giulia parked around the corner from the Prince's mansion in the heart of Chelsea. They were outside a church with a tall spire, shielded from CCTV by a Land Rover in front of them and a white van behind. Bonnie leaned into the back footwell for her rucksack. She removed a tiny bottle of prosthetic adhesive from the front pocket and painted it around the edge of her mask. The ritual helped her get into character. Stealing might be in her blood, but it wasn't in her nature. Bonnie, The Thief, was a role she played; an act that gave her the freedom to do what was necessary.

Her task tonight was to relieve the controversial Prince Ahmed of his rare pink diamond. Not that it was ever technically his. He took ownership of the raw gem from a family of jewellers in Africa during a royal visit. He smuggled it into the country before having it polished by a disreputable jeweller here in London. Bonnie assumed that when you're raised to believe royalty is your birthright, it's second nature to help yourself to whatever you please. She couldn't relate; she'd been taught throughout her childhood that she had no birthright due to her one, albeit massive, indiscretion of being born female.

Growing up, the girls in her dormitory treated her like she was lower than the other kids at the school. She was, after all, only there because her father was a teacher. Bonnie never corrected that assumption. Never let them know that her family had held an earldom in Scotland since the Norman conquest and that her grandfather was one of a long line of hereditary peers — she didn't care enough about their opinion of her to explain herself. Bonnie wanted to make friends who liked her for who she was, not the zeros on the family bank balance or the titles in front of her name. Her family made their more recent fortune through patenting a design for a lock-box that still graced many household safes; her surname was on every other lock and house key in the country. The irony was never far from her mind on nights like this.

"Earbud," Giulia said, handing it over. Bonnie pushed it into her ear. "Testing, testing."

"Ow. Feedback," Bonnie confirmed, wincing at the echo.

Giulia muffled the microphone with her hand. "Okay, it's a tight squeeze past the church, but once you're out the back, there's open space. Keep to the trees. I left a mark on your best option, it's right where you need to be. I'm already in the security system so say the word and I'll deactivate the alarms."

"Second skylight, right?"

"The triple one, not the double. You can anchor yourself to the chimney stack, it's sturdy enough. When you leave, come out via the gate for the playing fields. Martin will bring the car around for you. You ready?"

Bonnie blew on the edges of her mask with a flourish. She doubted it had any effect on the pros-aide, but it was something to do while she waited for it to get tacky. "We've gone over this so many times, I could do it in my sleep."

"Well done, you just jinxed the job. I hope you're proud of yourself." Giulia shook her head and made the sign of the cross while Bonnie laughed.

"'Plans A through Z', remember?" Bonnie pressed the mask to her face, carefully holding it in place until she was sure it was stuck fast. "How do I look?"

"Like Goldilocks got mixed up with a bad crowd."

"Perfect, let's do this."

"I'll be at the bus stop across the road, so I'm close enough to cause a diversion if you need it. Please don't need it."

As Giulia strode around the corner towards the bus stop, Bonnie pulled on her backpack and glanced up the street in all directions, checking for overlooking windows and CCTV cameras before scurrying between the church and the neighbouring building. On the other side, she found the promised open space, a stretch of manicured lawn next to a blaize football pitch. The whole area was bordered by oak trees, one of which had a yellow paint mark on the base of its trunk.

The trunk bisected just above head level. She pulled herself up with her fingertips until she was able to clamber ungracefully into the branches — zero out of ten for style. Fortunately, Dhruv wasn't around to appraise her efforts. The thickest part of the trunk led her to a spot almost opposite the chimney stack she needed. She was a little to the left and there would be an incline to reach the roof, but all that meant was she could return more easily when speed was of the essence. On the way in, stealth was her priority.

Bonnie unfolded the limbs of the crossbow and aimed for the lowest point she could see on the chimneystack. When adrenaline surged, it was harder to aim; fight or flight fought between themselves for dominance. She took a calming breath, refocused her aim and squeezed the trigger. Martin's bolt design used an anchoring system that gripped the bolt in place using four metal spikes that extended when force was exerted on the rope. Once the bolt hit home, she tugged the rope taut, feeling resistance. All she had to do now was secure her end with a bowline and attach the utterly useless safety lanyard to her harness. Only the offchance of losing her footing would ever make this useful —if either anchor gave way, she'd smash into the ground or the side of a building. With that reassuring thought, Bonnie lay on the rope and began to commando climb across the gap.

Pigeon-deterring spikes lined most edges of the flat roof. Anti-climb paint was added behind that, almost as an after-thought, most likely at the behest of the insurance company. Londoners, more afraid of pigeons than burglars, go figure.

Sweat pooled at the base of her spine and her scalp itched under its layers of wig and wool cap. Perhaps the real hair wigs would be less uncomfortable, but the idea of accidentally leaving somebody else's DNA at a crime scene brought her out in guilty hives. On the roof, she unhooked herself from the rope and was securing the next one in place when a panicked Giulia sounded in her earpiece. As a rule, they maintained radio silence unless totally necessary. Hearing her voice now didn't bode well.

"Uh, Bon? The security system has been deactivated."

"That was the plan. Why do you sound surprised?"

"I didn't do it."

Bonnie glanced into the gallery in time to see a shaft of light flood the room as the door opened. Bonnie leaned back from the chimney stack, letting the rope take her weight; it was secure. Silently, she opened the skylight and watched the figure approach the diamond. Her diamond.

Shit. I did jinx it.

Through the fog of surprise and indignation at somebody else taking her diamond (okay, not hers but her feelings were valid), she formulated a plan. Somewhere in Jim's 'A through Z' was a solution.

"We have company, Giuly. Would you be so kind as to re-activate the system? I need a silent alarm, please."

"Done. I have eyes on the gallery door, the guards are a minute away."

"Can you give me a ten-second countdown when they get close?" Bonnie balanced on the ledge and lowered herself through the window onto a hefty rafter below. The harness took her weight before she let go. Gripping the rope in her braking hand, she leaned back and as the mechanism lowered her to the ground.

"10, 9, 8, 7..." She landed on her tiptoes between the man and the diamond. Panicked brown eyes widened at her appearance. Stifling her amusement, she raised a finger to her lips; if the guards outside heard them, the game was over. Bonnie coiled herself around him, feeling the strength in his thighs and the definition in his chest. A burst of citrus, spice and musk hit her nose and her focus drifted from the job for a split-second. Thieves should not smell this good. In other circumstances, she'd be trying to get him out of the sharply tailored tuxedo he was wearing. "6, 5..."

"Hold on." She hit the controls on the wristband of her glove, and the motor burst into life, lifting them upwards. At the first tug, his arms tightened around her, and her cheeks flushed warm at the closeness. With two of them, progress to the roof was slower than usual. She desperately hoped they'd reach it in time.

"4, 3, 2, 1. They're coming in."

The door burst open and a handful of guards spilled into the room. Bonnie stopped the mechanism where they hung in midair next to the rafter. She could chance it and swing them over, but the risk of dropping him was too high. That thought made her tighten her grip. She simply had to hope nobody looked up. It was a mild night; the harsh winter had finally melted into spring. There was no wind or rain to attract attention to the open skylight. Her arms started to ache. She hardly dared breathe. Every moment the guards spent searching the gallery increased their chances of finding her and her new acquaintance dangling from the ceiling. Why were they so thorough?!

Eventually. "False alarm!"

"We need to get the geeks in to fix the system, it's still glitching."

Relief washed over Bonnie and she smiled. Giulia had been playing with the network for a week, undoubtedly responsible for the glitches. It was a useful way to explain a shutdown like they had planned for tonight. Until the attractive stranger changed the plan.

When the door closed and streetlight was the only illumination in the room once again, she finally let out the breath she'd been holding and started their descent. His back was to the diamond when she released him. By the time he'd regained his balance, it was in the palm of her hand.

She let him study her, safe in the knowledge that little about her was distinguishable — taking her chance to do the same. Aside from the black leather gloves, everything about his appearance suggested he was here for the party. His dinner jacket was unbuttoned, bowtie loose, and his hair fought against its perfectly styled coif. There was an undoneness about him that was, well, sexy. His eyes shone more bewitchingly than the precious stone she held behind her back. Flustered was a good look on him, she hoped it was as becoming on her.

"Thank you," he said, voice low and breathless.

"It's nothing. Maybe you can repay the favour sometime? Something tells me our paths will cross again."

Before he could respond, she activated the controls and pushed back to avoid kicking him in his handsome face as she was lifted from the ground. She swung back and landed cleanly on the rafter long enough to stow the diamond in her jacket pocket, before pulling herself up on the ledge and out through the skylight, shutting the window carefully. Then she removed her ropes from the pulley system and stuffed them into her backpack, silently thanking Martin for his genius with gadgetry. If he hadn't automated her rappel system, her escape tonight would have been too slow.

The gentleman thief in the gallery below could still be down there watching her exit, or he could have raised the alarm. If it was the latter, Bonnie didn't want to hang around. The effort of the incline on the rope earlier paid off now, it made an effective zipline. She clipped the karabiner on and skated towards the tree, hand over hand, defying all safety messages Dhruv had ever impressed on her. The anchored bolt released from its mooring with a twist and a tug — a movement unlikely to be replicated during careful use. She bundled that into her backpack, too and began her ascent from the tree. She spotted her exit when her feet soundlessly hit the soft grass below. Maintaining stealth, she stuck to the shadows to reach the gate and climbed over it. Earlier today, the playing fields would have been floodlit, not now. She ran across the middle, to the next gate and exited at the same moment a blue Corsa pulled up next to her. Martin reached behind him and opened the back door. He was moving before she fastened her seatbelt.

Bonnie pulled off the beanie and impatiently peeled the blonde wig away from her hairline. She shoved them and the wig cap into the front pocket of the backpack and tried to ruffle her hair into some kind of volume. Two hundred metres later, he stopped for Giulia in front of a dark alleyway. Bonnie ducked down in her seat. They chose the location because it was a CCTV blackspot, but she wasn't keen on taking chances.

"That was close," Giulia said.

"Too close." Bonnie replayed the scene over in her mind. Where had he come from?

Giulia opened the glove compartment and retrieved some of the adhesive remover wipes they kept there and tossed them back to Bonnie. Mind occupied, she started to remove the mask, working slowly around the edges until the pros aide finally gave way.

"What happened back there?" Martin asked, brow furrowed in concern.

"Bonnie had company."

"Security?"

"No. Another thief. He was already there when she reached the skylight. If we hadn't set off the alarm, he'd be home free right now."

"Shit. We knew the diamond was sought after, but what are the chances someone else would take it at the same time as us?"

"Slim to none. Someone must have known we were lifting it tonight." Giulia's fingernails drummed against her messenger bag.

A piece of adhesive was caught in a tuft of hair by Bonnie's temple. She rested her head against the car window as she worked the sticky clump to the ends of her hair. Her mind raced. She wasn't used to having company on these jobs, least of all somebody else targeting the same item as her. Was Jim's information compromised? Were his connections talking to other thieves? Why tonight? Above all of her questions, one loomed more significantly than the rest. One that Martin spoke aloud for all of them.

"Who the fuck was he?"

Martin dropped her off on the edge of Hyde Park, and she walked the last ten minutes to the townhouse, all the time, turning Martin's question over in her head. Until Giulia set off the silent alarm, he'd been poised, self-assured. Even then, he had enough experience and awareness to feel the signs that something had been triggered. It wasn't his first job. Why was this the one to bring them together?

"Bonbon! Come in. It's too late for a young woman to be wandering the streets alone."

Bonnie shook her head at him. Jim would gladly send her into dangerous situations and let her risk arrest for him, but his protective instincts kicked in as soon as she dared walk outside after 11 PM without an escort.

"I can look after myself."

"I know. That doesn't stop me worrying about you. Tell me, were you successful?"

If the police thought they knew who was behind the thefts, Bonnie was sure they didn't have the image of a grey-haired man in a cardigan and carpet slippers in mind. As criminal masterminds went, hers was more affable than the stereotype. She followed Jim into his wood-lined home office, dominated by an ornate antique oak desk. It was too large for the space which only emphasised its size even more. Jim squeezed in behind it and sat in the anachronistically jarring desk chair. Anything with ergonomic lumbar support was out of place in the time-capsule he called a study. Bonnie rummaged in her backpack for one glove and pulled it on before she unzipped her jacket pocket and removed the diamond. It gleamed in the yellow light of the office lamps.

"I almost wasn't, though."

"Oh?" Jim was inscrutable at the best of times, but Bonnie thought she saw the flicker of a smirk on the corners of his mouth. Did he know something? It was his contact who let them know that the Prince was planning to move the diamond and when it would be most vulnerable. Did Jim know more than he was telling?

Yes. Jim had more secrets than most. They were currency to him. For every fact he told her, she assumed he was concealing three more.

"There was another thief there. You knew that was possible, though, didn't you? That's why we had to act tonight?"

"Something like that, yes. Tell me about this other thief."

"He was..." *Handsome? Fragrant?* "... Professional. If we hadn't diverted him, the diamond wouldn't be on your desk now."

"Well, I don't know about that." That smirk again.

His bullish attitude could have been a mark of his confidence in her abilities as a thief, but, with Jim, there was always more to it. Perhaps, she just needed to believe that he trusted in her skills and had all the logistics in hand. It was easier to think of him as an amiable puppetmaster than a fallible man.

"Jim? You've got this under control, right?"

"Always, Bonbon." He jumped up from his seat and started pacing. "I was going to make a midnight snack, do you want to join me?"

Bonnie checked the time and groaned. Jim's midnight snack was more than an hour overdue. She had a meeting in the morning, and home was at least twenty minutes away. "On two conditions," she said. "One, you make cheese on toast, and two—"

"The spare bed is already made up for you. Come on, you can grate while I toast."

"Thanks, Uncle Jim, you're the best." A swell of gratitude towards the man broke, and she hugged him.

"I know." He kissed the top of her head. "But don't tell the others, they'll get jealous."

2

The barista drew the line at four shots of coffee in one cup, so that's what Asher clutched to his chest as he took his seat at the conference table. When he left the party at midnight, he knew sleep wouldn't come quickly. He was still awake when his mother called at 3 am, upset and anxious, needing to talk to someone. After an hour of reassurances, she finally calmed down enough for him to let her hang up, letting him catch a couple of hours of rest before his alarm signalled the start of the day. Without palpitation-inducing levels of caffeine, he wasn't going to get through the day. Especially when that day was a Monday.

Another morning spent listening to his father's most trusted department heads sucking up to the man while Asher stayed silent, waiting for his own chance to impress him. Another afternoon analysing pointless data into reports that nobody would ever read.

In amongst the same old faces around the conference table, Asher spied a new, pretty one. Dark hair fell loose in waves around delicate features and familiar blue eyes. He felt as though he already knew her, except that he'd have remembered if he'd met her before—he was good with faces. She was alert and ready for business, yet completely relaxed. In this room, surrounded by so many egos, she knew her worth. Asher was staring, but he didn't care. Not until she caught his eye, then heat unconnected to his enormous cappuccino spread over his cheeks, he had to look away. He felt her gaze on him, curious and intense as he tried to focus on the notepad in front of him.

"If everyone is here, we can start," Galvin said. Every person around the table sat up at attention. Almost everyone. "Miss Duncan, would you like to introduce yourself?"

Several people sat forward, Galvin didn't give anyone else the floor so early in a meeting, and they wanted to know who this woman was. Asher was amongst them. For her part, she seemed utterly unfazed by the attention. Twirling her pen between her fingers a few more times, she rested her forearms on the table.

"Hi, you can call me Bonnie. I'll be managing your social media accounts from now on." Her smile was on just the right side of smug. Confident and assured but without conceit. Asher instantly liked her.

Her accent was Scottish, but beyond that, hard to place. If he had to guess, he'd favour east coast over west, probably central. Sometimes, living in England for a number of years softened an accent, blunting the hard edges until a geographic location was impossible to pin down. It happened to his grandfather, too. By the time Asher knew him, there were only mild residues of Spanish left, certainly nothing more precise than that.

"Excuse me," Kieran Reuter, chief commercial officer and head of the Galvin Anderson Butt-Kissing Society interrupted. He addressed Galvin, not Bonnie. "I didn't realise we needed any help with our social media accounts. We haven't had any issues without her."

Galvin opened his mouth to reply. Bonnie spoke first. "No, you haven't had any issues, largely because you've been inconspicuous. For such a prominent company, your social media presence is pitiful. Meanwhile, boutique chains and independent hotels that you would never have considered as competition a few years ago are growing organically through superior social media strategies. If you want to stay in the past and dismiss an avenue that's proven to grow your business, fine, but Mr Anderson recognises the potential opportunity."

Kieran's ears turned red and his eyes narrowed as he glowered at Bonnie. She looked utterly unconcerned that she'd made an enemy. If Galvin noticed the exchange, he chose to ignore it.

"Why don't you tell us what you have in mind for us, Miss Duncan."

"So far, there's nothing wrong with your social media presence as such. It's just... Flat. You show lots of beautiful images of your hotels and their interiors, and that's certainly appealing, but your engagement is poor. I want to do something about that by telling the stories contained within your hotels. Your excellent events teams create the most amazing weddings, balls and birthday parties. Let's show some time-lapse video of the setup process so people can admire the hard work that goes into that. The people who work in customer-facing roles in your hotels are the real heroes of most guests' stays. We can showcase them, celebrate them." She was addressing Galvin, but she had everybody's full attention. "I want to work with select influencers, use CTAs and strategically boost and sponsor posts to grow your profile. I want people to think of Anderson Hotels first when they travel."

The heads of the chief officers for events, human resources, customer service and marketing were bobbing in agreement.

Bonnie might have lost Reuter, but she had the approval of Jackson, Campbell, Clarke and Goulden. Reuter had reached the top by backstabbing and brown-nosing, he was surely only one slip-up away from being exposed. The other four were universally liked and all were there on merit; Duncan had made good allies, whether she knew it or not.

"Miss Duncan will be with us three days a week so all department heads should book time with her. Over the next two weeks, she'll be gathering all the information she needs to transform our socials into something noteworthy. If you don't have your diaries with you today, call Gabi in PR, she'll be able to fit you in." Galvin's eyes rested on Kieran at the word 'all'.

Socials. Asher guessed that the current Mrs Anderson (a woman old enough to be Asher's younger sister) was likely the cause of Galvin's sudden interest in social media. Anderson's sixth wife was a model and had millions of Instagram followers. Before meeting her, Asher would have put good money on his father not knowing his apps from his elbow. Now, it was his priority.

Galvin moved to the next subject on the agenda and Asher turned his attention to his coffee. The dry business of customer satisfaction surveys and unionising chambermaids ploughed on labouriously. As each department head reported on their successes, his eyes were drawn again to the new girl.

Her phone was laying on the table next to a dictaphone, green light blinking. A tablet in a bulky case sat next to those. On a notebook, she added to an intricate spider diagram with swooping, slanted writing. Asher could see a quick mind working behind eyes, which, the more he examined, seemed tired, weary. Would she want to speak to him about his department?

Data administration was hardly tweet-worthy; Asher knew better than anyone that the role of Performance Analysis Manager was created for him. Nepotism will take you anywhere, unless you're Galvin Anderson's child, then it got you a tedious, made-up office job. Galvin had never asked for Asher's input at one of these meetings; his opinion didn't count.

Somehow, the meeting wrapped up in a timely manner. It was unusual for them to finish before lunch, but today, Galvin called Any Other Business by eleven-thirty, by midday, they were done. As everyone packed up their notebooks and phones, a queue formed in front of Bonnie. Asher watched her calmly address each one in turn with relaxed confidence, selecting a time slot with them and noting their office location and details required to gain access to the building. Kieran Reuter, Asher noticed, did not book an appointment.

Finally, Bonnie began to pack her own things away and Asher loitered in the hallway outside, pretending to check his phone. The deep hum of voices in the meeting room told him that Galvin was doing most of the talking. Before he could wonder what they were discussing, the door opened. Asher felt like a rabbit in headlights. It was obvious he'd been eavesdropping.

"Asher can show you around, Miss Duncan. I'm afraid I have other business to attend to. I hope you settle in well."

"Around?" Asher asked, caught off-guard.

"The offices, Asher. Give Miss Duncan the lay of the land, as it were."

"Thank you, Mr Anderson." Bonnie smiled and shook his hand. Galvin gave them a curt nod and strode down the hallway and into a waiting lift. *Sure, dad, I don't have anything bet-*

ter to do. It was a stark reminder that his role here didn't mean anything.

Bonnie misread his expression and looked contrite. "Asher, right? If you have something better to do, I can live without the guided tour."

"Oh, no, it's not that. Come with me." He put his hand on the small of her back and directed her to the elevator. "If we're going to do the full, official tour of Anderson Hotels HQ, I'm going to need fuel. There's a deli across the road. Lunch first, tour later."

With a half a passable Reuben and an oversweetened iced tea in his stomach, Asher felt almost human. Almost ready to impress. He leaned forward, elbows on either side of his plate.

"Tell me about yourself, Bonnie Duncan."

"Not much to tell, really. I moved to London at seventeen and lived with my grandpa. When I started university, he made me move into halls of residence, 'it's not an authentic experience if you don't live in halls'. He died when I was nineteen, and my uncle gave me a job with him. I... ended up running his social media accounts, amongst other things. After uni, I kept working for him, as well as helping out on some campaigns for small businesses and local charities. That led to corporate jobs. I now run accounts for several companies, charities and influencers. That's it." She shrugged.

That's it. Asher didn't buy that. She hadn't told him more than her CV could. There was more to this woman than met the eye. She had an assuredness about her that spoke to stories she was choosing not to tell. Yet. If there was one thing he was good at, it was getting that kind of story out of people.

"Where did you move from?" He asked before taking a crisp from his plate and tossing it into his mouth.

"Scotland." He shook his head. Not good enough. "All over, really, my father's job took us to different places but Helensburgh originally, then Elgin and Perth. I moved here just before they moved to Clackmannanshire. As far as I know, he, my mother and brother are still there."

He swallowed thickly, barbs of potato chip scratched his throat. "As far as you know?"

"It's a long story. Actually, it's short but it not a first meal together kind of story. Raincheck?"

"I'll hold you to it. How was your lunch?"

She prodded the remnants of her club sandwich. "It was good, thanks. So, what's your story?"

"Homeschooled. Well, I was seldom home, my dad took me with him wherever he went and my tutor came, too. He wanted me to have an Ivy League education, so that's what I did. While I was there, he divorced his third wife and married my tutor. After university, I started working for him and—."

"That's it?"

Touche. "My mother is ill. After my father moved onto wife number two, she had a breakdown and tried... Well, she was in a bad place. She never really recovered. That's why my father brought me up."

"I'm sorry." Her hand now rested on his where it lay on the table next to his plate. He smiled the forced smile he'd been taught to wear whenever his mother came up.

"It is what it is."

She took a drink and looked thoughtful. "I don't think it is. As children, of whatever age, we expect our parents to be there for us. When they can't be, it hurts. You don't have to be flippant about it, it sucks."

"It does suck." The nights he spent talking her through the latest panic attack, the days worrying about the fact that she hadn't called. Wondering if she would ever get better, coming to terms with this being her 'normal'. Anger at having his mother stolen from childhood memories by mental illness. Helplessness at not being able to fix her. Frustration at sharing the financial burden of her private care with his uncle now that his father had washed his hands of her. All of it wore away at him, and his father didn't care, she wasn't his problem any more.

A stray tear dropped unbidden from his eye. One that missed the regular lectures from his father about stoicism and 'getting on with business' being the thing that would help his mother most, not emotion. He should have tried to hide it, but there was something about her, he didn't want to hide anything from her — almost anything.

She squeezed his hand, and he felt more understood by her than any of the legions of therapists and counsellors his father had insisted he see. Asher didn't know the cause of the decade of distance between Bonnie and her parents, but he knew enough to feel her empathy in this moment.

"Okay," he said, wiping his cheek and inhaling deeply. "Let's go do this tour."

"Are you sure? We can do it another time?"

"Positive." He wasn't.

"Why don't I get us coffee, and you can grab some fresh air?"

He bobbed his head, feeling another lump in his throat. She understood that he needed to compose himself and was sensitive enough to give him some time alone to do it. In an office full of his father's cronies or people too afraid of the boss to befriend his son, he had finally found someone he could relate to. Assuming she felt the same way.

There was one way to find out. Bonnie emerged from the coffee shop with a cup in each hand.

"Thanks." he accepted his coffee and grasped it with both hands. "So, this is weird, we just met, and I'm not presuming anything, but, do you want to come over to mine tonight? Friends only, obviously. Takeout and a boxset?"

It took all of his effort to not say 'Netflix and chill'.

She breathed sharply through her teeth. "Tonight is no good, I have to do something for my uncle."

"Oh, no problem." He struggled to keep the disappointment from his voice. Until she turned him down, he hadn't realised how much he wanted to spend more time with her.

"Does tomorrow work?

"Yeah." He grinned. "Tomorrow is great."

Asher stopped short of doing a happy-dance and attempted to conceal his joy behind his coffee and promptly dribbled it down his front. *Smooth, Asher, very smooth.*

Fortunately, something further along the pavement was interesting her more than he was. Her eyes were focused on a point to the right of his face and a half-smile spread across hers. It was a knowing look, as though she had remembered a private joke. Asher had a sense of deja vu but didn't dwell on it. He turned his head to where she was looking and saw a newspaper vendor on the corner of the street. The headline was in bold print in an A-frame in front of the man's stall.

DARING DIAMOND HEIST: PRINCE'S PRIZE GEM PILFERED.

"Nice alliteration," she said, nodding towards the vendor.

"Yeah." He was still sore that he had his prize snatched away from under his nose and was beating himself up about it. He knew he owed the mystery woman a debt, without her intervention, he'd probably be a headline himself, but he was bitter that she managed to take the diamond like she had. He fully intended to meet the light-fingered woman in black again and next time, he'd be on top.

"Were you there?"

"Why would you ask that?!" Asher heard his voice quaver at the suggestion.

"At the party?" Bonnie clarified, "You're something of a society darling, no? I expect you're invited to events like that one all the time."

"Oh, yeah. I was there." Asher's panic dissipated as quickly as it rose. For a moment, he thought he'd been caught out. "Nobody at the party knew what happened. I don't think the Prince even found out until everyone had gone home."

"Shame. I thought maybe you met the thief." A mischievous sparkle gleamed in her eyes.

Asher laughed resentfully. "I wish."

Bonnie hummed in acknowledgement before draining her coffee cup. She sashayed towards him until she was only a dozen centimetres from his face. Asher swallowed thickly. She was close enough that he could count the freckles on her nose. She aimed her empty coffee cup over his shoulder. He turned in time to see it land in the bin, several feet away.

"Now, Mr Anderson-Diaz, shall we start that tour?" She asked, her voice low and tantalisingly familiar.

3

If she'd had to imagine her first day at work for Anderson Hotels, Bonnie would never have predicted it would come the morning after she had the boss's son between her thighs. Typically, a guy like Asher would leave her flustered, but knowing she had the upper hand on him the previous night was all the confidence she needed.

For one heart-stopping moment, she thought he recognised her, but his interested gaze passed in a look of bewilderment. He was disarmingly charming, and it was easy to forget the circumstances in which she first met him. By the time they had finished lunch, they were two new friends learning about each other, not two thieves trying to catch each other out. Only that headline managed to break the spell.

She shouldn't have teased him about it. It was risky. He could have recognised her eyes or her voice once she'd given him context. She couldn't help herself; it was too much fun to toy with him. If his reaction told her anything, it was that he wasn't used to being asked about that part of his life. He worked alone.

What drove a rich, successful young heir like Asher to steal priceless diamonds in his down-time? What did he have to prove? Uncle Jim didn't have children of his own, and she was the only one who could carry on the family legacy — did Asher have a similar obligation?

"Asher Anderson-Diaz, are you sure?" Giulia couldn't get her head around the news. "He seems so... Predictable."

"Are you looking him up?" Bonnie was careful to keep her voice low. The tiles were designed to absorb sound, but she wasn't taking any chances.

"I am now. Wow, that is one good-looking dude, no wonder he's all over the celebrity gossip blogs. He's a ladies man. There are dozens of photos of him with an array of different women on his arm. And a kiss and tell or three. Oh! She's from Made in Chelsea and that one was on Love Island."

"Wonderful. I suppose he is easy on the eye, and his father's a confirmed playboy, I guess the apple doesn't fall far from the machismo-strewn tree."

"You know, we could use that to get close to him, find out what he's planning. I'm sure you could have a meeting of the minds, womaniser to womaniser."

"Rude." Bonnie wasn't a womaniser. Not deliberately, at least. She found it easy to meet women and was a natural flirt. Hooking up with bi-curious pillow-princesses came easily; finding someone who wanted to love her was more difficult. After Lucy, she needed to feel wanted, casual sex was easier than another heartbreak.

"The truth hurts, Bon. All I'm saying is you have lots in common: a penchant for grand larceny, you're both wealthier than Scrooge McDuck and you've both got game..."

"Actually, I have one X-chromosome too many to inherit any of my family's fortune. As far as I understand it, Asher doesn't get a penny either until he takes over the company. He's well remunerated for his job, but as far as the Anderson coffers go, they're sealed shut until Asher's the new CEO."

"How do you know that?"

"Galvin told me. The plan is for Anderson Junior to take over the company in the next ten years so that Anderson Senior can retire to the Caymans with whomever the current Mrs Anderson is at that moment in time."

Giulia snorted in derision. "Still not refuting the philandering, I notice."

"I don't think females can even be philanderers, Giuly."

"Let's ask Shona or Debbie what they think. Even better, we could ask Whatsit and Thingie, the ones whose names you didn't bother to learn if they think the term applies to you."

Bonnie wondered if she should mention the week she spent with Adam or her one-night stand with Trevor but rejected the idea. It furthered Giulia's argument more than hers.

"We're meant to keep lines clear for essential coms only, you know?" Martin interjected. Through the tiny earbud, Bonnie practically heard Giulia roll her eyes, and she grinned. Martin could always be trusted to keep them all on message. "Giuly's right though, you are a womaniser."

"Hey, you're meant to be on my side!"

"I'm here to be impartial. In this case, I can't be, I've seen you at work."

"Speaking of work, I have a safe to crack. Can we focus on that, please?"

Sweat ran up her forehead and into her hairline, the muscles in her legs threatened to cramp as she clung on to the bars of the dropped ceiling and lowered herself into the room below. The CEO's office was locked and out of bounds so Bonnie had to access it through the ventilation system. Once in the ceiling, she was stuck there — the floor sensors around the safe were separate from the main security system, and Giulia couldn't disable it remotely, so she had to make like a bat and hang upside down. The wall safe had been installed into the brickwork in the 1950s, and the B&D offices were built around it two decades later. Old and sturdy, the CEO saw no reason to change it for a newer model which suited Bonnie just fine.

After the previous night's interruption, she would have preferred to case the building more thoroughly. When Jim had called her about the job, she couldn't refuse; the opportunity to grab the USB stick came up suddenly, and they had to act. Now that she had her hands on the safe, Bonnie was starting to relax. The combination felt like it hadn't changed since the safe was purchased seventy years ago, the notches were so deep she could feel each one with the tips of her gloved fingers. Usually, she'd have to feel the wheel's movement with her bare hands and would require complete concentration for this type of job — not tonight.

"Have you got the numbers for me?" Martin asked, ready to run the combinations.

"5, 9, 11, 27, 48 and 53."

"Tonight's machine is Guenivere, and we're using set of balls number four. There are seven-hundred and twenty possible combinations of those numbers. Giuly, can you narrow that down?"

"Thank you, Martin, tonight's jackpot is worth a cool thirty million pounds and many future jobs, so fingers crossed for everyone at home."

The lottery skit was as much a part of the ritual as Giulia's pre-job pep talk and the obligatory supper and debrief with Uncle Jim. It was annoying, and Bonnie wouldn't change a thing.

"None of this is essential coms," Bonnie said. "Meanwhile, I'm getting dizzy."

"Well, the original business opened its doors on the twenty-seventh of May, 1948 and the owner was married on the fifth of September 1953, so I've just narrowed your options down to two. The safe was installed in '55."

Martin chuckled. "Which was most important to the owner, I wonder? Love or money?"

"According to their granddaughter's Facebook album, the couple celebrated their sapphire wedding anniversary last year. my bet's on love."

Bonnie turned the dial six times to the right before she stopped on five. The wheel dropped when it hit the mark. She held her breath and turned the dial back towards the nine, feeling relief when it dropped too. The rest followed in the same way; the combination was well used.

"Giuly was right on this one. Love wins over money," Bonnie said, pulling the bolt upwards and swinging the door open. The flash drive was exactly where Jim said it would be, on the top shelf of the safe, resting on a sheaf of papers bound with elastic bands. Bonnie unzipped her jacket pocket, tucked the memory stick inside and zipped it back up. Before the safe door swung closed, she replaced the drive with a matching blank one, selecting it from a bunch Giulia gave her earlier. She let the door close with a 'clunk', pushed the bolt to and gave the dial a quick spin.

The 1930s office building was renovated in the 70s, and as such, the high decorative ceiling had been obscured by suspended acoustic tiles. Bad for architecture, good for Bonnie. The plenum space was only just deep enough for her to crawl through. It was mercifully light on wiring and pipes. She needed to reach the neighbouring office, where the extra security measures didn't extend. CCTV covered the hallways, but nobody was watching. Security disabled the alarms and took a break while the cleaners did their rounds.

Her eyes had adjusted to the darkness in the roof space, and now, even the dimly lit office was a sharp contrast. Bonnie pulled the cleaner's tabard on over her head and picked up the basket of cleaning products she'd left there. All she had to do was get to the exit without running into the shift supervisor.

"Do you have eyes on the corridor?" Bonnie asked.

"All clear," Giulia said. "They're on the other side of the building now. Before you go, can you pick up something for me from the reception area?"

"If you need paperclips, I can recommend a good stationery store." Bonnie pushed the office door open a crack to check the hallway before striding towards the foyer.

"Not paperclips, no. Just pick up what's on the printer."

Bonnie abandoned her tabard and basket of cleaning products, reached over the reception desk and retrieved the contents of the print tray, dropping it into her back pocket before heading back towards the automatic doors. They opened without ceremony and she stepped outside, feeling a familiar tension in her gut. No sirens, no flashing lights. It didn't matter how many times she did this, Jim had trained her to expect the worst. *'Until you have exit plans A through Z, you're not ready for the job.'*

Outside, Martin flashed his headlights at her from his place at the edge of the car park. She worked her way towards it around the edge of the expansive lot, mindful of the security cameras posted atop four pillars at each corner. Giulia had knocked the cameras offline, but Bonnie skirted the boundaries of their field of vision regardless. You could never be too careful.

The engine was already running so Bonnie hopped into the passenger seat as Martin put the car into gear.

"Did you get everything?" Giulia asked from the back seat. She patted the front of her jacket where the memory stick was still stored. "And the card?"

Bonnie retrieved the plastic item she took from the printer from her back pocket and passed it to her. Giulia slipped it into the breast pocket of her jacket without explanation. Bonnie looked at Martin, who shrugged, he was in the dark, too. It wasn't unusual. Uncle Jim liked to segment information.

The lights on the M40 passed by with hypnotic regularity. Bonnie's eye started to feel heavy. She wasn't sure when she fell asleep, all she knew was that when Martin nudged her awake, they were in London.

"Bon? Do you want me to hang around and drive you home afterwards?" Martin asked.

"No, you guys get home. Thanks, though." Bonnie dragged herself from the car, feeling the chill in the air deep in her tired muscles.

Uncle Jim was waiting for her at the door, ready to usher her into the office. Bonnie passed him the flash drive before curling up on the armchair in the corner of the room.

"Thank you, Bonbon. Any problems?"

She shivered and shook her head. "None. Your information was spot on, this time."

He smiled thinly and placed the USB stick in the top drawer of his desk. He patted the leather-lined surface above the drawer. "This should confirm a few things, tell us what as well as who. Not just about the watch — other items, too."

"Are we on the right track?"

"I believe so. Your surveillance will tell us that for sure. How did it go this morning?"

Bonnie shrugged. "It's early days, but I arranged meetings with heads of departments and got a tour of the building. I'm starting to get my bearings. Incidentally, the tour? It was from the same man who was trying to rob Prince Ahmed last night." She observed Jim as he absorbed her news. He was inscrutable.

"Quite. Giulia told me. It's interesting, to say the least. These meetings, will they be useful?"

"I should be able to get what I need. Some of them are meeting me in coffee shops and restaurants, others at HQ and a couple of the hotels in the city. It won't take more than a week to get everything. There's one minor problem."

"Yes?"

"The commercial director doesn't want help from a whippersnapper like me, certainly not with social media. He's being obstructive." Petulant was more accurate. Kieran Reuter was the kind of man who didn't like being told he was wrong about anything. She recognised the type — rigid and unwavering.

Jim nodded knowingly. "I'm not surprised. Keep your eye on him if you can."

"And the other thief? Asher Anderson-Diaz. What do we know about him?"

"I know quite a lot about him, don't you worry. I hear he asked you out?"

She shook her head. "As friends. Anyway, I just got out of a relationship."

"A year ago, Bonbon. It's time to move on."

Tears pooled in her eyes. Time should heal all wounds. It didn't. It was never easy to know she was unwanted.

Jim opened the bottom drawer of his desk and pulled out two tumblers and a bottle of whisky. The 1990 Bruichladdich single malt was distilled in the year she was born, and Uncle Jim claimed he was saving it for a special occasion. This didn't feel like one. "Some things require cask strength spirits. Broken hearts are one of them."

She took the glass gratefully and sniffed the amber liquid. The sweet, woody smell was deliciously comforting. When she arrived unannounced at her grandfather's door, over ten years ago, he wrapped her in a knitted blanket, poured her a generous measure of whisky and listened without judgement as she explained her side of the story. Without question, he took her in. Now, as the peatiness coated her throat with reviving warmth, she felt the same acceptance. Uncle Jim understood.

"Even if I was ready, I can't 'move on' with Asher. I'm an employee of Anderson Hotels now. They take a grim view on inter-departmental relationships."

Jim chuckled and leaned back in his chair. "Since when have you been a stickler for the rules?"

4

Her arms ached. Dhruv was working her extra hard, and she knew her limbs would punish her for the exertion in the coming days. Over time, she'd grown to rely on Martin's automated rope system which made her lazy. They knew that not every job would allow her to use it, and Dhruv was determined to correct her overreliance in the cruellest way possible. They started on the 5.11 wall. It was pushing Bonnie to the limits of her skill.

"There's no rope on this next job, Bon. It's you versus a second storey window; you need to be sharp."

Frustration and pressure were making it harder than usual to keep her footing.

"Oh, buggering fuck! I can't do this." Bonnie was, once again, dangling from a rope.

"You're highly strung today, Bonnie." Dhruv was enjoying this too much. "What's up?"

"Haha, you're hilarious. Can you let me down, please?"

Dhruv's shit-eating grin shone up at her as he lowered her back to the ground. If she could have reached, she would have been tempted to kick him in the teeth on the way to the floor. "For real, though, Bon, what's on your mind?"

She dusted her hands with more chalk, nursing her aching fingers. So many thoughts were running through her mind that it was hard to pick the one that was distracting her most. "Things are complicated; that's all."

"More so than usual?"

"Let's recap. I'm currently spying on my new colleagues while trying to do my actual job which, considering they had absolutely no social media strategy and the last person to handle the company's accounts was a summer intern, is no mean feat. Meanwhile, the boss's son is jaw-droppingly gorgeous, interested in me and I happened to bump into him the other night, mid-B&E, while I was Mission Impossible-ing it into the private gallery of an African prince. He asked me out and I'm going to his after training tonight with no idea what I'm doing. It's been years since I went on a date, how will I know if this is one? Besides, I can't date him, he's a coworker. Oh, and I have to go to my ex-girlfriend's place the day after tomorrow for a briefing for the third job in a week even though I'm still not really over her and whenever I see her I want to beg her to take me back. So, yeah, Dhru, more complicated than usual. "

"You're going to his? Tonight?" Dhruv squealed.

The laugh that took over started in her knees and worked its way up until it forced its way out her mouth in a burst. Hands on her thighs and doubled over, the ridiculousness of his reaction in response to her situation struck her almost overwhelmingly. Dhruv stared at her, perplexed, until the laughter petered out.

"Feel better?" He asked.

She did. Her pent up tension had dissipated, albeit temporarily. It was enough to allow her to focus on the climbing wall. She found footholds more easily and accessed more power in her fingers. She was close to reaching the top.

Dhruv waited until Bonnie was ten feet off the ground before he started the questioning. It was playing dirty but she couldn't blame him, she'd done the same thing to him in her past. You had to play along when the person interrogating you was literally holding your life in their hands. The unspoken rule between them was that belayer picks the topic of conversation so they often used the opportunity to have frank talks about things they'd usually avoid.

"Is this guy you're seeing the one from the diamond job? Martin and Giuly convinced you to go out with him, then?"

Of course they were taking credit for that; they continually laboured under the illusion that they dictated her love life. It was the problem with such a close friendship group — everyone felt a certain level of ownership over the others' relationships.

Bonnie called down to Dhruv. "First of all, I'm not 'going out' with him. Those two have oversold it to you. It's a friend thing. Secondly, he asked me before the job at B&D last night, so nothing either Martin nor Giuly said made any difference,"

"Sure."

"Stop smirking."

"You can't see my face."

"No, but I know you, and you're definitely smirking."

She and Dhruv had been close friends since day one of freshers' week. They shared every secret with each other. He stood by her after her grandfather died and her family turned on each other, joined Uncle Jim's crew at the same time she did, encouraged her to do her first job. She even introduced him to his husband. There was no lying to Dhruv, he knew her too well.

"You like him, don't you?"

"There's something about him that's compelling," she admitted. "He's not who I first thought."

"I'll bet. This 'something about him', it's more than just his being a jewel thief?"

"Failed jewel thief." She heard the gloating note in her voice before she could censor herself. Best to get it out now, she thought. Yesterday afternoon had been a test of sheer willpower, she so wanted to rub it in his face. She was a bad winner.

"Careful, you know what pride comes before," Dhruv said and tugged on the rope, dislodging her from the wall.

She looked down from where she hung and glared at Dhruv's smug face gazing back. "You're a dick, you know that?"

"Speaking of dicks, what time is your date?"

"Eight-thirty, why?"

Dhruv hastily lowered her to the ground where she landed inelegantly in a heap. "Best get going, then."

Bonnie untangled her limbs and removed her harness, leaving it for Dhruv to sort out, before running towards the locker room. She would have enough time for a shower, assuming the buses ran promptly between the gym and Asher's part of town. She could do her makeup on the bus.

Usually, the warmth and comparative tranquillity of the shower cubicle was a place to linger, but she was too on edge tonight. Why had she agreed to this so readily? Asher intrigued her beyond their less than conventional shared pastime. She wanted to get to know him but at what cost? Dare she risk exposure? She shut off the water and reached for her towel. Everyone wanted her to get close to Asher: Dhruv, Martin and Giuly might have her romantic interests in mind, but Uncle Jim's concern was purely professional. What was his motivation?

Still in her towel, she padded out to the empty climbing hall. Dhruv was coiling rope beside the storeroom. He looked up as she held out two dresses. "Pick one."

"Not the black. If it's not a real date, then you shouldn't be too dressy. Save it for the fourth not-date." He pointed at the teal one. "The peter pan collar is cute, and the colour brings out your eyes. Wear it with your Converse — it'll be more casual."

"Thanks, bro." If only his life advice was as sound as his fashion advice.

The doorman let her in through the full-length glass doors, and she tried not to notice the points of access. The entry system was operated by NFC, but the housing of the controls would be easy to pick. Likewise, the lifts; the doorman used a key on a chain on his waist to call the elevator. A quick photograph on her phone and email to Martin, and she'd have a 3D printed copy in her hands by the end of the night.

It was hard to turn off that part of her brain and simply enjoy the moment instead of continually casing the room.

The doors opened at Asher's front door; his flat took up the entire floor. She stepped out and knocked. He answered quickly, wearing stonewash jeans and a white linen button-down shirt with the top two buttons undone. It was more casual than she had seen him yet, but it suited him. He looked very, very good.

"Sorry I'm late."

"Come in." He smiled and stepped aside. "How was your workout?"

"Hard work." She grimaced as her muscles reminded her of the difficulty level of that wall. "Everything hurts."

He ushered her through the hall, into a large open-plan living room and kitchen. Polished marble blended into plush cream carpeting and grey upholstery. Nothing in the room gave her insight into Asher's personality. It felt less like a home, more like a freshly opened showroom, unlived in and artificially tidy.

"Are you ready to eat?" he asked, "I was going to have something quick after work, then I got caught up doing other things."

Bonnie eyed the standby light on the console under his television, an abandoned controller under the sofa. She guessed that was what derailed his plans.

"I could eat. I went straight to the gym from work, then to here. I'm starving."

"Great. What do you feel like? Thai food? Hamburgers? Falafel? Grilled cheese?" He pulled a stack of takeaway menus from a kitchen drawer. She assumed delivery apps had rendered the takeout drawer obsolete, but Asher was clearly a traditionalist.

"If you're making me choose." He nodded at that. "Then Thai food sounds amazing."

"Any preferences?"

"Surprise me."

After he phoned in their order, Asher called the doorman to warn him that he was expecting a delivery. Glass of wine in hand, Bonnie admired the kitchen. The appliances were state of the art and virtually unused. She remembered when she renovated her kitchen and blew most of the budget on a five oven dual fuel Aga. Dhruv laughed at her for installing something so middle-class in a student kitchen, but it became the heart of her home. Bonnie and her friends spent most of their time in the house in that kitchen. Even now that they'd all moved out to their own places, it was still a popular place to hang out. Some days, she'd come home from work to find her friends were already there, uninvited. Given their shared criminal proclivities, there was no merit in asking for the spare keys back; they'd still find a way in.

She wondered how Asher spent his free time.

"Sorry for the mess," he said, redundantly. The room was spotless. "My cleaner is on holiday. The place will look much better by Friday."

"Just in time for weekend entertaining?"

"I don't entertain." He looked at her sincerely. "I do get invited to parties, but aside from my cleaner and food delivery people, you're the first person to see the inside of my flat. When I'm not working or networking, I'm... Well, there's not much time left."

"Oh, I heard you were a ladies man."

She said it without thinking, assuming that he'd be proud of his playboy reputation. She was wrong. He winced, looking hurt by her words.

"What makes you say that?" He looked wounded — she immediately regretted saying it.

"My friend, Giuly. She googled you." *Well done. Bonnie, you sound like a crazy stalker.*

"That's Galvin's fault. Everyone expects it be like father, like son. It's not. Despite what the gossip blogs suggest, my sexual exploits have been greatly exaggerated, I promise."

"I'm sorry. I should know that online and real life are different things. That's my fault."

"It's ok." He assured her. "I... I searched for you, too. There's very little to find, I was quite disappointed, to be honest."

That was by design. Aside from a professional website and blog and a handful of private social media accounts, there was little clue to her identity online. Part of the reason was her desire to obscure the past. She didn't need Zsa Zsa Stukley-Heatherington III and the like looking her up and reporting back to their peers and, ultimately, her parents. Mostly, however, it was a precaution against being found out — limiting her online presence kept her inconspicuous.

"So, you didn't find out about my own womanising?"

Wine came out of Asher's nose. He choked. "Pardon?"

"As much as I try to refute it, my friends insist. I had a rough breakup last year, and I've been wallowing in my singlehood by having meaningless sex."

Why are you telling him this, Bonnie? This. Is. Not. A. Date.

"With women?"

"And men. Although not at the same time." *Okay, Bonnie, time to stop talking.*

He nodded slowly. In her experience, awkward silence was as good a reaction as she could expect. He didn't get angry, tell her it was just a phase and kick her out the door. In Bonnie's books, that constituted a win.

His response was lost in the sound of the door buzzer. The food had arrived. Hunger compounded the nervous turmoil in her stomach, and it rumbled in response to the prospect of dinner.

While Asher answered the door, Bonnie looked around for crockery. It was helpfully stored in a glass-fronted cupboard with the cutlery in a drawer below. Most of the utensils were pristine, some still had tags on them.

"How long have you lived here?"

He counted on his fingers. "Uh, five years. Since I got back from the States."

They fell into effortless synchronicity in the kitchen, passing plates to each other, serving food, pouring drinks. Considering they were technically rivals, they worked well together. He set the dishes on the counter while she served the rice and curry. Asher suggested they eat on the sofa, so she carried both plates while he transported drinks, cutlery and napkins from the kitchen.

Small talk came naturally as they ate. Bonnie felt as though she had known Asher for years, not days. She regretted that she couldn't tell him about their coincidental side-hustle, had to remind herself that he was still a stranger.

"I like your ring," he said, pointing to her right hand where gemstones glittered on her ring finger.

Reflexively, she turned it with her thumb so that the sapphires and diamonds faced her palm. It felt ostentatious and she preferred to display the platinum band. "Thanks, it was my grandmother's."

I would have also inherited her Marquessate if it wasn't for The Incident. One of the few titles to pass through the female line before the Downton Law, her grandmother became Marchioness after her own father's passing. It would have eventually been Bonnie's, much to her brother's chagrin.

"Has Gabi shown you her engagement ring yet? Her fiance went to Dubai for it. I hear it cost £30,000."

It was the first thing Gabi did after introducing herself. The engagement was recent and the glaze of excitement was yet to wear off. Bonnie had smiled and celebrated with her, but her expert eye noticed that the ring wasn't as advertised.

"No, it didn't." Asher's eyes widened and she saw her rudeness reflected in his expression. She rushed to explain herself. "I just mean, yes, it's almost 4 carats, and maybe if it were internally flawless, I'd believe it, but it's not. There's a cavity inclusion near the upper girdle facet that will chip in no time. If that's really what he paid, he was conned."

"How do you know so much about diamonds?" Asher's eyes narrowed.

Shit.

She smiled brightly to conceal the lie. "I don't really. I made that up, was it convincing?"

When you steal a few good ones, you start to understand what quality looks like.

"No, you didn't. My Uncle Rami is a jeweller. He taught me a few things, and that was spot on."

"Oh?" Rami. Uncle Jim had a poker buddy called Ramirez who taught her how to appraise stones. He gave her a loupe for her birthday one year.

"Yeah. When I was at university, he was working for a jeweller in Boston, so we would meet up and go to card games. I learned a lot from him. So, how do you know so much?"

Her brain was freewheeling, she couldn't think of a believable response. "Uh, I did an Instagram campaign for a diamond jeweller once." *Please don't ask for the name.*

"Okay." He didn't sound convinced.

It was hazardous, feeling close to someone like him. She forgot that he didn't know everything about her. Worse, it could be dangerous for her to reveal that side of herself to him, no matter how much she wanted to. Until she knew she could trust him, she had to be more careful.

"So what were you playing before I got here?" She asked, trying to change the subject before she gave away too much of herself.

He eyed the abandoned controller and smiled. "Very observant. I was playing Mortal Kombat. You play?"

"Not for a very long time. We had a console in the house at university although it was mostly the boys and Giuly who played."

"You lived in a house share?"

"Of sorts."

It was her grandfather's house. He left it to her in his will, although her parents contested that. Uncle Jim ensured she got what Grandpa intended her to have and helped her pay the inheritance tax. It was just another thing she owed him. The whole affair succeeded in making the rift between them and her parents even deeper; irreparably so. The idea of living alone in such a large house terrified her, so she begged her friends to move in. It was a more appealing option than the cell-like halls of residence or an overpriced flea-pit nowhere near a tube station — they all gladly accepted the offer.

Bonnie had gone from a dormitory to her grandfather's house, to halls of residence, then back to the house with her friends. Communal living had been her life. Until Lucy moved out, she'd never been alone. Now that she had tried it, she wasn't sure she enjoyed solitude.

"That must have been fun. I had a single room at uni. I've never had a housemate."

Is that why you work alone?

"If you don't mind regular invasions of your privacy, yeah, it's fun," she said. Then she remembered her climbing session with Dhruv. "Actually, with my friends, the invasions of privacy aren't dependent on a shared living space. They're always butting into my business."

"That must be nice."

The longing in his voice hit her emotions hard. Asher was lonely. She had an urge to hug him. "Mortal Kombat, then? Shall we play?"

Asher grinned and took her empty plate from her, casting it aside on the coffee table. He handed her a controller and woke the system with his own.

"Choose your fighter," Asher said and selected Liu Kang. Bonnie flitted between Jade and Kitana, unable to decide between them. She eventually settled for Kitana, her usual choice.

"Got a thing for leather-clad women in masks?" He asked.

"Don't we all?" She quipped, trying to hide a smirk.

"Yeah, well, they're not always who they seem."

Asher was good, much better than her, but like most gamers, he had tells. When he concentrated on certain combos, his tongue stuck out of his mouth, wedged between his teeth. Bonnie knew when he was about the deliver his final attack because he'd raise himself off the seat in preparation to jump up in celebration. By observing him, she was able to figure out his technique. She played conservatively, waiting until her opponent's energy was low enough to launch a final assault.

She waited and lost a few more matches until she was confident in reading the signs. When she saw him starting to rise from the couch, she struck before he could and finally won.

"No!"

"Yes!" She cheered. "In your face!"

She jumped off the couch and pointed at him, goading him. She was a terrible winner, but the victory was so satisfying she couldn't help it. Asher's arms were crossed, his face puckered in a fake huff, but his eyes sparkled and betrayed his amusement at her childish display. She stepped forward to do, something, but quickly forgot what. The area rug was uneven where they'd jostled each other, bumping the sofa across the carpet and Bonnie tripped. Asher reached out to break her fall and, together, they toppled onto the couch

"Oh my god, I'm so sorry."

"No harm done, are you okay?" He asked.

She was on top of him, her body pressed to his, their noses almost touching. Yet, she made no attempt to stand up. There were so many reasons why she should move; he was her boss's son, workplace relationships were forbidden, she was hiding a massive part of her life from him, and, come to think of it, he was keeping secrets from her, too. Some force was keeping her there, and she struggled to fight it.

"I should go, it's getting late," Bonnie said. She still didn't move.

"You could stay?"

She whimpered. She knew she'd have to be the level-headed one and leave. Every fibre in her body was crying out, begging her to reconsider. "I can't. We can't. I just signed the policy about sex and relationships and the workplace."

"Oh, that? No, that policy forbids sex *in* the workplace. The cleaners didn't like the extra work. Right here, on the sofa, is fine."

"Nice try." She giggled. She put her hands on either side of Asher's shoulders and pushed herself up, grateful that he was so good-natured about it all. Other guys might accuse her of leading him on.

"Can I call you a taxi?" He offered.

She shook her head, "Thanks, but the fresh air will clear my head."

Bonnie didn't know why, but as they waited for the lift to arrive, she heard herself blurt out, "the reason why Google didn't tell you anything, by the way? That's because you searched for the wrong person. My real name is Bonameah Fitzduncan. I changed it when I moved to London."

"Bona-what?"

"Yeah, good luck with that." She winked and grinned as the lift doors closed between them.

Once she was alone, she leaned back against the mirrored walls and groaned. What had she done?

5

Detective Inspector Felicity Stewart surveyed the room. It was a crime scene, but it was unlike most she'd seen. For starters, there was no damage. Most thieves were less considerate, damage to property was part of the deal. More frustratingly, there was no obvious point of entry or exit. The one door to the gallery was covered by a secure keypad, and the skylight was at least twenty feet up. If the plinth bearing the Prince's diamond wasn't empty, she would be asking why she was here.

Her promotion to Lead Detective on the Organised Theft Taskforce was proving a dubious honour. Her workload was enormous and seemed to increase daily. The network of thieves, burglars and con man in the city was extensive and trying to join the dots and finding the men and women pulling the strings was close to impossible. A product of the Detective Fast Track Programme, Fliss was motivated to prove her worth. She thought she'd proven herself during her stint in CID, but this taskforce felt like a step back. So far, she had succeeded only in failure.

It hadn't escaped her that the initials for her team were OTT. Today's crime scene was a frustrating reminder of that.

"Hi, I'm looking for DI Stewart?" A distinguished-looking man hovered by the door.

"That's me."

He blinked slowly and shook his head. "Sorry, I'm just checking my male privilege. I was expecting a man."

"Don't apologise, you're not the first. At least you have the self-awareness to recognise it. Most don't."

"My apology stands, it's not a good first impression." He looked like he was mentally kicking himself. She felt sorry for him.

"Do you want a do-over?" She asked.

"Please. Hi, I'm Carl Perez, you must be DI Stewart?" He grinned and strode towards her, hand extended.

She laughed and shook the proffered hand. He was charming. Up close, she could see that his black suit and monogrammed briefcase were designer; he was too sharply dressed to be law enforcement.

"Nice to meet you, Carl, you can call me Fliss, everybody else does."

"In that case, my friends call me Rez. I'm an investigator for Brache & Debar Insurance. I believe you and I are investigating the same crime." He fished an ID card out of his pocket and flashed it at her. "Prince Ahmed's missing diamond. My bosses are putting pressure on me to recover the item, so I hoped we could share resources."

"Well, Rez, if it helps me solve the case, I'd be happy to. Fair warning, though, so far all I have is dead ends. There's no security footage, no fingerprints, no clear point of entry. Nothing."

Rez's look of consternation mirrored her feelings. This wasn't the first case she'd worked that ultimately went cold due to a complete lack of evidence.

"Not their first time, then?"

"No. There's a string of unsolved, high ticket robberies in my filing cabinet and I'd be willing to bet that the person who did this is behind a few of those crimes too."

Most criminals were opportunists, and seldom smart enough to pull off something this seamless, she had to be dealing with a serial burglar. It was frustrating. This taskforce had every potential to become the most demoralising job she'd ever had, and she once worked traffic. If working with this insurance investigator could help her finally catch a thief, she was willing to do it.

Rez shrugged nonchalantly. "Okay, tell me what you've got. We have to start somewhere."

"We've got nothing," she admitted. "The crime scene techs have just left empty-handed and I was about to do the same thing. Feel free to have a look for yourself."

"The alarm didn't go off?"

"It did, actually. Apparently, the system's been glitching all week and went off several times during the past few days. The guards checked the gallery every time and found nothing suspicious. The only way to get in here without activating the alarm is with a security pass and all are accounted for."

Rez inspected the empty plinth and the floor surrounding it. He gazed up at the skylight then rotated on the spot, taking in the rest of the room. Fliss wondered if that was how she had looked earlier today: clueless.

"What about CCTV? There must at least be something covering the street outside? A local business, anything?"

"Uniforms are on it. I'm not hopeful."

Nothing about this case gave her hope. She expected to be filing it with the others by the end of the month.

"Is there access to the roof?" Rez asked.

"The boundary has two gates, both with keypad entry, both covered by cameras. There's an eight-foot-high wall with metal shards set into the concrete at the top around the rest. If you get past that, you've got spikes and anti-climb paint on every window ledge and the edge of the roof."

"So, no."

Fliss laughed. At this point, it was that or cry. High profile victims like the Prince were entitled, impatient and fond of complaining to the press when their case wasn't solved immediately.

"Inspector?" Detective Constable Arif Maamoun stood in the doorway, clutching a tablet. The collar of his shirt was stiff and his jacket was slightly too large. He looked like his mother had dressed him. Arif was recently out of uniform, his discomfort still showed.

"Can I take some photos?" Rez asked and waved his phone at her.

"Help yourself." He started to snap the plinth and its surroundings while Fliss turned her attention to DC Maamoun. "What have you got, Arif?"

He turned the tablet screen towards her and hit play. Grainy, black and white CCTV footage showed a female dressed in black, complete with stereotypical burglar mask, disappear into a gap between two buildings. The camera must have been mounted high off the street because little detail was distinguishable. Fliss could make out fair hair under the hat, beyond that, there were no features that would make a usable description.

"I've watched the video through for a few hours. She doesn't reappear." Arif chewed his lip, his eyes darting from the screen to her face.

"Why do you look so concerned?"

"Ma'am, look at the date on the footage. This isn't from last night, it was the night before."

Fliss blinked. "Are you saying the diamond wasn't stolen yesterday? Why didn't they notice it was gone for, what, 48 hours?"

Over her shoulder, Rez spoke. "I have a couple of suggestions about that. To be completely honest, I was surprised Ahmed even let his people call the police."

DC Maamoun stared, open-mouthed at Rez until Fliss remembered herself.

"Sorry, Arif, this is Mr Perez from Brache & Debar, Rez, meet Arif Maamoun, the Detective Constable on my team." The two men shook hands cordially. "What do you mean?"

"What do you know about the diamond?" Rez asked. His stance changed from controlled to defensive.

"It's pink, expensive. Larger than your average engagement ring." She shrugged.

"It arrived in the UK uncut. From a country not certificated by the Kimberly Process."

Fliss stared at Rez. She had no idea what he meant. Fortunately, Arif did.

"It's a Conflict Diamond?"

"Exactly. My company insured it after it had been polished and, ostensibly, we didn't know its history, but the prince was cagey about its provenance so I dug a little deeper. As I understand, Ahmed was planning to sell the gem, which is why he reached out to us."

"For a valuation," Fliss said.

Arif's voice cracked when he asked, "how much?"

"For something with the clarity and colour like the Prince's, £50,000 a carat. This one was six."

Arif whistled through his teeth. Fliss felt sick. The responsibility of recovering the diamond weighed even more heavily than before. Its suspect origins warranted investigation, but her task stayed the same. Find the thief, find the diamond.

"No pressure, ma'am, but we really need a win on this one."

You don't say, Maamoud. "Quite. We should go for a walk and see where our thief went."

Rez nodded. "Let's go outside."

The gap between the buildings was tight. The broad-shouldered Maamoud had to turn sideways to fit through. At the other end, Rez brushed brick dust off his jacket. Behind the street, the space opened out into a park and playing field. A well-kept football pitch and lawn lined with trees, concealed from the general public. Fliss could imagine the nearby office workers coming here for a quiet lunch away from the bustle of the street. In the summer, it would be busy. Now, in a cold early spring, they were the only three people here. She scanned the area, looking for security cameras, hopeful for another clue. Rez wandered around the edge of the grass, eyes on the ground.

"Yellow paint." He pointed to the base of a tree trunk "None of the others have it."

Fliss looked around. He was right. The tree in question was directly behind Prince Ahmed's mansion. Her eyes followed the trunk upwards. She tried to picture the most obvious path up the tree. There were higher branches but one, roughly halfway up, stood out to her. It overhung the back garden, taking any climber within reach of a second-story window.

"Arif, can you make sure the crime scene techs come back and check around here?" Maamoud nodded and got on the phone.

It hadn't rained in days, but Fliss felt the heel of her shoe sink into the recently thawed ground. She inspected the area under the tree, searching for patches of bare earth until she found what she was looking for. A metre out from the yellow splodge was a clear impression of the tread of a boot. She pointed it out to the others.

"Good catch." Fliss was used to male officers patronising her for her abilities, but Rez seemed genuinely impressed. Her ego swelled at the compliment.

Arif took photographs on his phone and marked the spot with a little yellow flag. They would stay there until a technician could come back to collect the evidence. Rez wandered to the other side of the gardens and looked towards the house, shielding his eyes from the sun. If he noticed anything, it was unimportant.

"I should go. Paperwork waits for no man," he said and held his hand out to her.

She shook it enthusiastically. "Thank you for your help, I'll keep you updated if we find anything new."

He fished a business card from his lapel pocket and passed it to her with a wink. "Likewise."

Arif watched him leave with a smirk. "With respect, ma'am, he's got at least ten years on you."

Fliss ran her tongue across her teeth, swallowing a retort. She looked younger than she was —yet another reason her superiors underestimated her— so Arif might be off-base with his estimate. Rez, on the other hand, had the look of a man with wisdom beyond his years. The grey hair skewed things, too. If she had to guess, she'd have put the age difference at closer to five years. Not that it mattered.

"With respect, Arif, I'm not sure what Mr Perez's age has to do with anything."

Arif's grin was pure insubordination. "Well, this is the first time I've seen you smile and I think it has everything to do with him."

Sometimes, DC Maamoud's keen observational skills were a curse.

6

The mingled smells of linseed oil and turpentine filtered down the dim stairway. Olfactory memories of holidays by the sea at her grandparents' house washed over her. Grandma would set up on the beach and paint while Bonnie and her brother hunted for shells and pebbles that resembled sharks' teeth. Half the time, Grandma had to cling to the canvas to prevent the wind from blowing it away. Bonnie and Henry made a game of finding the biggest rocks on the shore to anchor the easel into the sand.

That was the house she stayed at every school holiday. The only place she'd felt like part of a family. Her father's eternal disappointment that he had borne a girl-child first was subsumed in every interaction they had, and Bonnie felt compelled to justify her existence through accomplishments. Her grandparents didn't care. They loved her and Henry for who they were, not for their potential to honour (or disgrace) the family name. At their house, Bonnie was free to be herself. Perhaps it was no coincidence that the two places that felt like home to her, her grandparents and Lucy's studio, had the same aroma.

Lucy opened the door, waking Bonnie from her reminiscences. Forcing herself back to the present, she greeted Lucy and stepped inside. Streetlight glowed through the large windows that lined one side of the room and gave everything a yellowish hue. The opposite wall was adorned with portraits, including some of Bonnie that made her look significantly more beautiful than she saw herself. In the centre of the room, an easel bore a flawless replica of a Sophie Van de Berg oil on canvas that Bonnie had only ever seen in books. A still life of flowers and insects that was studied in creative arts classes as an example of flawless composition. One of her photography lecturers had a print on the wall of his office, overlayed with a Fibonacci spiral, the image below perfectly fitting the ratio.

"Lucy," Bonnie said. "It's beautiful."

"It's just a copy, nothing special."

"Don't say that. You don't just forge or copy a painting, you recreate it. You capture the soul of the artist."

"Well..." Lucy started to remonstrate before deciding against it. "It won't be fully dry for a few more days so it's not finished yet. As rush jobs go, this one is cutting it fine."

"Where's the original?"

"Bought by a private collector on the outskirts of the city. It fetched £550,000 at auction last week."

Bonnie whistled, impressed. She stepped back to better view the painting and found Lucy in her path. Lucy's arms wound around her waist as Bonnie rested her head under her collarbone. The space was almost made for her. They weren't dating any more, not for some months, but the groove felt like it had been waiting for her. There was comfort in the embrace.

Although she had her own flat in Hoxton now, Lucy often slept in the studio. The bedclothes on the battered futon were rumpled; Bonnie guessed she'd pulled an all-nighter to finish the painting. Her breath hitched in her throat as memories of that bed reeled through her mind; she wanted to add new memories. Bonnie now understood why Galvin had a 'no relationships at work' policy — she was living with the awkwardness of the fallout of such a romance. The breakup was amicable. Being forced together like this, however, left a trace of tension between them that occasionally simmered over. Tonight, she was counting on it. After her near miss earlier this week, Bonnie needed to be wanted.

She turned to speak but the words were lost as Lucy's lips brushed hers. Frustration at recent events and desire to lose herself in another person drove her on, she tilted her head towards Lucy and kissed her. Lucy's hands moved to her waist and tugged on the base of her shirt. Calloused fingertips grazed her bare stomach and her muscles tensed involuntarily at the sensation. There was an ache in her core that, for once this week, had nothing to do with climbing strain. Soft lips moved down Bonnie's neck, teeth grazed her collarbone and lust flooded her senses. As Lucy grasped the hem of her shirt, Bonnie raised her hands above her head, assisting its removal. They stumbled backwards and fell onto the bed as one, Bonnie landing underneath Lucy.

Then, the image of Asher Anderson-Diaz swam into her head.

Go away.

She squeezed her eyes closed and tried to focus on Lucy, but he remained. His perfect fucking bone structure and stupid dazzling eyes were burned into her retinas.

Not now, I'm busy.

Imaginary Asher smiled and winked as Lucy's mouth found the curve of her breast. Suddenly, she wasn't in Lucy's studio any more, she was in Asher's flat, on his couch, underneath him.

"No. Sorry. I can't." Bonnie pushed herself to sitting. "It's a bad idea."

Lucy looked downcast but unsurprised. "If you're sure."

"I'm never 'sure', that's why we end up here time after time. We're better as friends, though. You said it first, you know why... "

Whether Lucy knew why or not was rendered inconsequential by the doorbell. Lucy got up to let Martin and Giulia in while Bonnie recovered her shirt and tried to regain her composure. The time it took the pair to climb the stairs was too short. When she walked in, Giulia's eyes moved ostentatiously from Lucy's flushed cheeks to Bonnie dishevelled clothing and tousled hair.

She arched one eyebrow. "Are we interrupting something?"

"Nothing we can't discuss another time," Lucy said, smiling conciliatorily at Bonnie.

"Sure." Guilia smirked and took four glasses off the shelf. She produced a bottle of wine from her bag and poured one for each of them. "Is this the forgery? Nicely done."

Lucy's face positively glowed at the compliment. Bonnie knew how much of her heart she poured into each artwork, original or replica, and how precious praise was to her.

"Indeed," Martin agreed. "Very accurate."

Bonnie sipped her wine and let Lucy enjoy the approval. Most of the time, Lucy's role was limited to appraising items after the fact and, as a result, she didn't always feel like she contributed to the crew's activities. When she was integral to the plan, Bonnie wanted to let her shine.

"When you're done grinning like a lunatic, we should get started," Giulia said pointedly.

Bonnie shrugged her assent. It took a lot more to embarrass her than pride in her friends.

While Martin and Giulia prepared their materials, Bonnie hopped up on the kitchen counter. Lucy joined her, hugging her wine glass with both hands.

Giulia pulled up a satellite image of a suburban area on her laptop. "This is Sevenoaks. Commuterville. Where £2,000,000 can buy you six bedrooms on the common and the local mums' group is more connected than the mafia." She zoomed into a large house on the corner of a green area. "It also happens to be home to one Kieran Reuter."

Bonnie reeled. She knew she would be spying on her new colleagues at this job, but breaking into their homes wasn't usually part of it. Man in the middle and keystroke injection attacks were guilt-inducing enough, B&E was a new low.

"Reuter bought the painting?" Bonnie asked. The role of Chief Commercial Officer paid well—multi-six-figures. Definitely enough to fund a mortgage for the house currently on screen. Enough to drop half a million on a painting, though? She wasn't sure.

"He's something of a collector." Giulia's tone was portentous.

"It certainly ups the ante on not getting caught." Something wriggled in her gut. It was as close to a conscience as she was used to these days.

"You need to cut as close to the frame as possible." Martin demonstrated on an empty frame propped up against an armchair. "Then place it on this plain canvas and roll it up, painted surface on the inside."

"I know, Martin. This isn't my first time." Lucy sniggered. Bonnie nudged her with her shoulder.

"In addition to that, there's the router you'll be carrying," Giulia said. "You need to position it behind the dormer roof on your way out of the home office. We can play with the signal from there."

"Tell me about the security."

"Nine-foot walls set with broken glass around the entire perimeter. The front gate has RFID keyfob entry and two cameras on a secure server. The house itself has a basic alarm system, motion, window and entryway sensors but it's only set when nobody's home."

"This isn't filling me with much hope, Giuly."

"That's because I forgot to mention the service entrance at the back of the building. That gate has a Symmons LX keypad entry system, the code is changed weekly."

Bonnie laughed. That was her exhaust port on the Death Star —every building had one— a vulnerability to exploit. The Symmons system was easily bypassed with a strong magnet. After all of the measures this mark had taken to secure his home, he'd slipped up by trusting that the sheer number of possible combinations was enough to deter someone from trying to get through the back door.

Martin held up a small device. "This is a powerful, very focussed EMP cannon. Aim it at the security camera above the service entrance and pull the trigger. DO NOT get in its path, the electromagnetic pulse will knock out your comms."

"Likewise my router," Giulia warned. "Keep all electricals free."

"What about the alarm system? How do we deal with that?"

"It won't be set."

Bonnie set her glass on the counter and shook her head. "But, you said it's set when nobody's home."

"Exactly."

Bonnie was no stranger to breaking and entering while the occupants of the building were there, but she wasn't usually entering a family home. The idea of coming across an errant child while doing her best impression of Burglar Bill gave her goosebumps on her scalp.

Foreseeing her objections, Martin spoke up. "The family will be out, they have tickets to a church concert. Only the housekeeper will be there, she's not allowed in the office."

"Okay," Bonnie said, starting to relax about the situation. "This doesn't sound too difficult."

Giulia grimaced. "You've got to stop saying things like that."

Bonnie let Martin and Giulia go on ahead, hanging back to catch a moment alone with Lucy.

"Is now a good time to discuss it?" Bonnie asked.

Lucy sighed. "Nothing's changed, Bon. The job always comes first for you; along with 'exit plans A through Z'. I need somebody who puts me at the top of the list, someone without one eye on the door, or the window."

It didn't get better, no matter how many times they talked about it. Family commitment was strong and Bonnie didn't have many ties left. She almost responded, but Lucy was right, there was no argument to be had.

"I get it."

"We're better as friends," Lucy said. "It hurts less that way."

Nothing had changed, Lucy was right. This job was her life. Her obligation. It meant she'd always hurt those closest to her in the end.

At the first landing, Bonnie sat on the steps and rested her head on the rough brickwork. Again, he faded into view in her mind's eye. Asher. By day, he had one life, by night, another. He must understand the stresses that brought, must know that daily conflict. If the job came first for him, too, could they find a balance? Was she fooling herself?

Would she always be making exit plans?

7

Asher couldn't push the woman in black to the back of his mind — she stalked his thoughts, mocking him. *'Something tells me our paths will cross again'.* She was sure their meeting wasn't a one-off, so what did she know? Asher frowned. He had relived the moment over in mind until it was all he saw when he closed his eyes. He must have triggered the alarm somehow, but how? The card he swiped should have disabled the whole system in the gallery. That was how the curator cleaned and maintained the pieces.

All week, he had sought answers. Instead, he met more frustrations, more questions.

His boss had been irritatingly sanguine about losing the diamond and Asher wanted to slam his fists on the desk in frustration until he listened.

"Fitz, what don't you understand? I was beaten to the punch by another thief."

"You win some, you lose some, my dear Asher. Consider it a lesson in humility." Fitz had laughed. "Tell me more about the other thief, I'm interested to know what you thought of her."

"There's not much to tell. The first I was even aware she was there was when she landed in front of me and saved me from security."

"Interesting. It sounds like she was a skilled operator," Fitz said to himself.

"Are you even listening to me, Fitz?"

"I am, yes. Perhaps you should have some support for the next job? A little back-up in case things go awry? I have an excellent gadget-man who can—"

"No. I work alone."

"If you insist."

Asher knew that Fitz had other contractors, he'd offered him assistance before, but he couldn't trust anyone else.

"There's a black market in just about anything you can think of. Spend five minutes on the dark web and you'll see for yourself the things people will trade illegally. The mind boggles. In every case, there are victims. Often, ones we will never be able to help. What we can do, however, is to stop the trade where we can and prevent further victims."

"Yes, sir." He knew this already, but the man was gearing up for an announcement and experience told him not to break his stride. Fitz relished a speech.

"I have recently come to possess a list. Items that have been informally insured by a company that chooses to overlook their questionable provenance. I believe that if we follow this list, we can find the major players." Fitz held a memory stick in his hand, waving it like a conductor's baton during his more passionate moments. "Before I continue, I need to know that you are loyal to the cause."

Insulted, Asher baulked. He had proven his loyalty time and again. "Do you even have to ask? After everything?"

"In this instance, yes. One of the names on this list is Galvin Anderson."

His lack of surprise was all the confirmation Asher needed. Galvin was a man who believed the rules didn't apply to the rich, Asher saw it in the way he treated his wives. In the way he treated him. Galvin had no time for remorse, that's what lawyers were for. A vertiginous sensation made him grip the arms of his chair. *Victims of the black market.* Asher was a beneficiary of his father's wealth; he was complicit.

"I'm in."

Fitz smiled warmly and nodded. "First of all, I need you to plant a bug for me. If all goes to plan, there will be an empty space ready for you."

Whenever he saw Bonnie, the thief and Fitz faded into the background, Bonnie's light was strong and he was inexorably drawn to it. He was starting to suspect that she felt something for him, too. That night, at his place, when she fell on him, she didn't immediately jump up. She seemed reluctant to leave, even. They had shared things with each other, things that were private, that they did want other people to know. He was sure he wasn't alone in disclosing details usually kept hidden.

Bonameah Fitzduncan.

That name. He tried various spellings before his search yielded results. Those results were almost as sparse as when he'd first looked up Bonnie Duncan, if more intriguing. Aside from a theatre review of a local amateur dramatic group which described her role in A Tale Of Two Cities as 'sparkling' and 'charming' and a mention on the honour roll of a prestigious boarding school in the highlands of Scotland, most of the results were from sites with names such as scotsnobility.org and peerage.co.uk. It left him with even more questions than answers.

There was more to her than met the eye; he was determined to be the one to uncover her secrets.

It was possibly the first time he had ever looked forward to work. It was definitely the first time he'd been nervous about it. He sat in the coffee shop across the road from the office and watched everybody file in, waiting to catch a glimpse of Bonnie. When she arrived, his heart leapt in his chest. She skipped up the stairs on light feet and stopped to chat to the security guards before heading to the lifts.

When he reached the door of the meeting room, he wondered if bringing coffee was the wrong call. She had the air of someone who was already significantly over-caffeinated. The pen in her right hand was weaving skillfully through her fingers which were in perpetual motion, the toes on her left foot were tapping arhythmically against the floor and her top teeth worried at her bottom lip, leaving white trails on pink. God, he wanted to kiss her. *Stop looking at her lips, Asher.*

"Hey, how are you?" *Stop staring, full stop.*

"Fine," she said. It might have been his imagination, but she looked at him accusingly. Did he do something wrong? Perhaps the annoying events of his own week were somehow bleeding into hers?

He slid the coffee towards her. "Hazlenut latte."

"I love you." She very definitely addressed the cup but Asher felt himself blush.

"So, uh, 'fine'. Actually fine or British-person-fine?"

She laughed and sipped her coffee. Her eyes fell closed and she moaned in pleasure at the taste. Asher was suddenly glad for the existence of the table.

"Better than British fine, worse than actually fine." Bonnie smiled and finally stopped twirling her pen. She set it on the table next to her tablet and turned her body to his. "Anyway, distract me from my fine-ness, tell me about you. What are you up to?"

"Not much. I spoke to mum yesterday and uh..." *I hung out with a criminal mastermind and plotted to extort one of my colleagues. You know, the usual.*

He was saved from explaining more by Andrew, Galvin's assistant. The nervous-looking young man knocked on the door frame and waited to be invited in. Bonnie waved him inside. He handed her a heavy ivory envelope before scampering back the way he came. She took it with a confused expression. It was addressed to 'Bonnie Duncan & Guest', written in exquisite calligraphy. Asher felt a moment's disappointment that it included the plus-one. Not that he could be her date, ever since Galvin made his secretary his third wife, fired her, divorced her and she sued the company for lost earnings, he'd taken a strict line on workplace relationships. Money was more important than love, especially to a man who viewed wives as expendable.

Bonnie tore open the envelope and pulled out the gold-embossed invite.

"It's the annual use-up-the-hospitality-budget-before- the-end-of-the-financial-year blowout. Execs, department heads and VIPs get to dress up, get drunk and feel important while the staff pull overtime to make it all happen." Asher explained.

"So cynical for one so entitled." Her lips twitched.

"I do apologise." He lowered his voice so that nobody in the neighbouring offices could hear him. "You would know entitlement, Lady Bonameah."

"Someone's been reading Debrett's, I see." Her face remained passive as her eyes scanned the invite. Asher reminded himself to never play poker with her.

"Yeah, well, you threw an alter-ego at me and left, you knew I'd look it up."

"I did. And I trust you to keep that particular piece of information to yourself."

"I will." Their eyes met in mutual understanding. He'd keep her secret locked away with his own. "Uh, are you taking a plus-one? To the ball?" His buttocks clenched in anticipation of her answer.

"I haven't decided if I'm going yet."

Asher laughed. "I doubt you have a choice. You'll be expected to cover it for social media." her head dropped to the table-top and she groaned. "Do it for the 'Gram, Bonnie."

"I hate you."

"No, you don't." He laughed. She turned to face him, one cheek still on the desk. Her eyes narrowed.

"I guess not. Who else will be there?"

"Everyone from the Monday meetings and their spouses, partners or mistresses. Everyone from PR. Any of the creative directors, executive chefs, graduate management rising stars and golden ticket holders."

She giggled and his heart fluttered to the rhythm. He imagined dancing with her at the ball, wondered what it would feel like to kiss her on the dance floor. He wouldn't be the one to do that, her plus-one would. Asher was already jealous of him or her.

There was nothing he could do about that. He could do something before that, though. The ball was a week on Sunday, maybe he could have her to himself this weekend?

"I know I keep doing the short notice thing, but are you free for a drink on Sunday night?" Asher was due to plant a bug that day. He could get back to the city in time for dinner, but it would be late.

"I... Yeah, I'd be free later on. I know a great place, give me your phone."

He hesitated before handing it over. Fitz had trained him not to trust anyone with his property, particularly items that could incriminate him. Asher was supervising. She was inputting her phone number, she couldn't do anything untoward.

"I'm out of town during the day, shall I text you when I'm heading back to the city?"

"I'm sure that would work."

8

The little coffee shop had a laid back atmosphere and a dim interior. Tables were squashed close together in the small seating area, but most customers were too engrossed in their own conversations to put them at risk of being overheard. Next to them, closest to the window, a mousy girl in thick glasses and a lilac beret sat in front of a laptop. Her head bobbed gently to whatever tune was being piped through her pastel-pink earbuds. Her fingers danced over the keys and her focus never shifted from the screen.

Rez rested his tray on the table, lifted off her latte and passed it to her. He placed a pot of tea and cup in front of his own seat and returned the tray to the counter. As he returned she saw him eye the neighbouring table and half-smiled as he read her screen.

"Do you want the good news, the bad news or the promising lead first?" Fliss asked.

He took his time, pouring tea into his cup and adding milk before he answered. "Let's start with the bad. It's all uphill after that."

There was a relaxed charm about him. Fliss wondered if he ever got angry. She was used to suppressing her own temper for fear of being labelled 'an emotional woman' in less than chivalrous circles and could recognise hot-headedness in others. Rez's conviviality wasn't forced. He was naturally calm. It wouldn't matter what order she gave the news to him, he'd take each with equal measure.

"The bad news is that our suspected thief disappears after her brief appearance on camera. To the point that we have no clue where she went. Half a million cameras in London and we only managed to catch her for thirty seconds on one of them."

"That is unfortunate. The image you do have, is it clear enough for a description?"

"It's grainy, it was dark. Honestly, she could be sitting next to me right now and I wouldn't recognise her."

Rez guffawed and spilled his tea. The girl on the neighbouring table passed him a stack of napkins to mop it up before he refilled his cup. "What of the tree? The yellow paint?"

"Generic spray paint. We'll never trace it. As for the tree. Our suspect might as well be a flying squirrel for all the clues we have beyond the boot impression. We assume they climbed the tree and accessed a window, but honestly, that's a guess. They could have morphed through the window for all the trace we have. All I do know is they've got balls. I sent a crime scene tech up there; he got cold feet and froze in place before he reached halfway."

Rez chuckled. "The intriguing question is, how did she get in that window without triggering the alarm? Flying squirrel or not, the glass was intact. She had to open it somehow."

"By luck or design, the glitching system probably let them in. We're still investigating what caused the issues. I'd bet it was no coincidence they got a false alarm in the moments before the diamond disappeared."

"Have you considered an alternate point of entry. I know the second-floor windows are the biggest and least secure but none of them lead to the gallery. The thief would have had to sneak through the building and we know the security team were active that night."

Fliss mulled it over. Occam's Razor led her to believe the most obvious solution, but since that hadn't answered her questions, perhaps it was time to think zebras, not horses. "You think they came in through the gallery window? There's no way. Unless the place was robbed by Spiderman."

"Not the window." Rez scrolled through his phone, turning it around when he found the picture he needed. "This skylight is directly above where the diamond was."

"Really? That's a sizable drop."

"If she made it from the tree to the roof, we can assume she had a rope. I think it would be remiss to write off this route based on the distance. You've already admitted that the thief is impressive."

It was as likely a scenario as anything else they'd investigated. She made a note to check with climbing gyms and outward bound centres for anyone with the level of skill required for such a drop. If she had time, she might visit a few places, interview any blonde ones.

She sighed and dragged a hand over her face. "Fine, I'll bring Spiderman in for questioning."

"It's all I ask."

Fliss laughed. She felt overwhelmingly grateful for him; his humour was a salve to her frustration. This was the first time her taskforce had more than minimal clues, thanks to Rez. He was her good luck charm. She almost said as much, but she remembered Maamoud's mocking tone when he pointed out the age gap. Rez had a job to do, he wasn't meeting her for personal reasons.

Feeling suddenly shy for no reason, Fliss picked up her coffee and blew across the surface of the cup. She concentrated on the foamy surface as she drank, admonishing herself for allowing Arif's comments to get to her.

"I have a question," he said. "You're saying 'they', but I thought you had established that the thief is a woman. The one on the CCTV? Is this a pronoun thing that I'm too old to understand, or has something changed?"

"Well." Nothing had changed, per se, but she was loathe to narrow down her options after only a fleeting glance at the woman. "The boot impression belongs to man's combat boot, so we've opened up the possibility that our female might have just been a Black Canary cosplayer taking a shortcut."

"That's fair." He leaned back in his seat, holding his teacup and saucer with perfect poise. He stopped short of extending a pinkie, although Fliss read somewhere that it wasn't accepted etiquette any more. A man like Rez would know that.

The boot print was her promising lead. It belonged to an obscure brand of footwear that only sold in a few boutiques in London and through a handful of authorised online sellers. DC Maamoun was cross-referencing credit card purchases with convicted thieves and known associates. If a name came up with ever the slightest link to organised crime, they'd be all over them.

"And you? Do you have any more information? About the diamond or who Prince Ahmed was planning to sell it to?"

"Ah, yes. The prince confirmed that he was planning to sell it via 'a contact'. That was, I'm told, the only person who knew he was going to move it."

"But?"

His grin widened. They were on the same wavelength. "A rock like that one? Rare and valuable. There's no way he didn't want a bidding war. His contact might have been one man, but there are at least two others who knew when Ahmed was selling it, I'd wager more."

At that, her pool of suspects widened from one fictional superhero, a grainy blonde female and a winged squirrel to three shadowy, but concrete, individuals.

"It gives me something to work with."

"Last we spoke, you were sure this robbery was linked to others. Have you found any others? Any of them insured by my company?"

"In for a penny, huh?" She laughed as Rez shrugged faux-innocently. "I have a series of robberies that appear to have taken place during or after special events at the location. Items taken from the venue or from guests by someone we assume was present at the party. We trawled through lists of in-house and events staff from every location for a common denominator, questioned a few people and even put the screws on the daughter of a mafia boss who's made it into the in-crowd. Nothing."

"It sounds like there's a lot of white noise to filter out."

9

The hefty industrial door was all security and no aesthetic. The original wooden affair, with its intricate cornicing and a door knocker that could anchor the Titanic, was starting to rot by the time she took over the house. A well-placed kick would have turned it into splinters. The functionality of the metal door suited Bonnie better, too. Few burglars would suspect that a home lay behind such a utilitarian facade. In that part of London, buildings such as hers were more likely to be used as a rehearsal space or yoga studio than for residential purposes. She enjoyed the anonymity.

Inside, beyond three high-security anti-snap locks, was her haven. Not a private sanctuary, however. Not if the two pairs of shoes in the hallway were an indication. Tattered white Nikes and pristine black Rothy's lay strewn across her welcome mat. Bonnie kicked them towards the skirting board before setting her own violet Vans neatly beside them.

"Hello, people who don't live here," she said as she reached the bottom of the staircase.

Giulia and Martin looked up from their laptops long enough to verify who she was, which was when she remembered her disguise. They had turned her kitchen island into a computer workstation, three laptops, some kind of wireless router and a forest of cables littered the worktop. In the limited free space, empty mugs were abandoned

"Hey, we're here, I hope you don't mind."

"I can see that, thanks." Bonnie removed her glasses and handed them to Giulia. "The battery is low on them, by the way."

"What did you find out?" Martin asked without taking his eyes off the screen.

"That I'm impressive. What? They said that, check the recording."

Giulia rolled her eyes as she plugged the glasses into one of a plethora of wires. "Anything we can use?"

"The police are still clueless. They don't have much and they're second-guessing the evidence they do have." Bonnie hung her beret and infinity scarf over the back of a chair and started to collect mugs. "You know, these aren't single-use. Rinse it and refill it, you monsters."

"Too much effort," Martin said. "Our brains have other things to do."

"I'm so sorry. I should have realised that. Since you're here, using my electricity and bandwidth, let me also clean up after you."

"Thanks."

She bit back a retort and didn't lob a mug at Martin's head. That would mean more mess. Instead, she dumped everything in the sink and ran the tap, holding her hand under the stream until it became warm.

"They are investigating the skylight as a point of entry. If I were them, I'd talk to climbing experts. It'll be worth warning Dhruv that he might get a visit."

Martin nodded, still focussed on his laptop. "So, no roof access for future jobs?"

"It's lucky I've been breaking my fingers on the advanced wall this week. I don't want to retire the gizmo yet, but it's best we take a break."

"Anything else?" Giulia asked.

"They have a boot impression and a CCTV clip of me on the street outside the church." A suddenly grey-looking Martin finally broke eye contact with his laptop to seek her assurance. "Nothing from the other side, though."

Cressida Dick might have decreed that the Metropolitan Police was no longer institutionally racist but Martin had no plans to test that theory in person. Bonnie might be the one committing grand larceny, but the black guy driving the get-away vehicle was likely to bear the brunt of the punishment should they ever be caught. The injustice made her blood boil while Martin remained resignedly impassive about the whole thing.

Bonnie washed the mugs, Martin and Giulia shared in-structions between each other. As hard as she tried to eaves-drop, the jargon rendered her attempts fruitless. As she placed the final mug on the draining board, she admitted defeat.

"What are you doing?"

"Setting up a relay server and a VM for the job tomorrow," Martin said.

"We need to remotely access the router you're planting for our MITM. We can use SSH tunnelling to do that, but we'll need to handle the firewalls."

"Shall I just pretend I understood all of that?" Bonnie asked.

"I don't have time to explain it so yes, please."

Bonnie spoke French, Latin and a little German. She didn't speak geek. Martin and Giulia could hold an entire conversation in acronyms while she, Dhruv and Lucy stood by in confusion. She understood the basics, where to plug them in and how to unleash them, she trusted the rest to her friends.

Martin turned his attention back to one of the screens as Giulia stood up, stretching her arms and arching her spine. She had doubtlessly been sitting in one position for hours. Bonnie pointed at the coffee maker and Giuly nodded enthusiastically. Her blood-caffeine levels were surely off the charts but Bonnie wasn't going to argue. She would sneak her some decaf later.

Bonnie inserted a pod into the machine and fired it up. The rich aroma of the steam reached her nose and turned her stomach. She'd been camped out in that cafe for too long, drinking too many lattes. Martin and Giulia might be able to drink the stuff endlessly, she couldn't.

Giulia opened the fridge and passed her the milk. When she shut the door, she plucked the ivory invite from its place behind a magnet of a Welsh dragon, a novelty gift from Giulia's parents.

"Who are you taking to this ball?"

Bonnie sighed, she didn't want to go but her attendance was mandatory. If she had to go, she wanted to take a friend, someone who'd make it fun. Her first choice would have been Dhruv, except he wasn't available and, logistically, he was less useful than his husband.

"I'm hoping Martin is free. He's the one who knows how the hardware works and he's so handsome in a tux." She raised her volume for the last part, staring at the side of his head.

"Flattery won't work. I can't do a decent lift. If you need backup, I'm no use."

"I'm offended that you think I'll need help on the lift. Honestly, it's like you don't even know me. I really need you for the cloning, Martin. I'd do it, but it's so much easier when there's a second person there. Would it help to remind you that Dhruv's family are visiting this weekend?"

He groaned. "When should I pick you up?"

Giulia passed the coffee to Martin as Bonnie set up the next one.

"Why aren't you going with Asher? I thought you two were a thing?"

"No inter-departmental fraternisation. Officially, we're not a thing. Not-officially, we aren't one either. We're friendly colleagues."

"That'll change after tomorrow, though," Martin said. Even when engrossed in his work, he was never deaf to the conversation.

"We'll see. I need to call Dhruv to help me pick out an outfit. When does he finish boot camp?"

"Couple of hours." Martin checked his watch. "We can help."

Bonnie snorted, glad she didn't have a mouthful of water. "I say this with the utmost love and respect for your individual skillsets, but neither of you has any sense of style."

Footsteps on the stairs announced another arrival. Black leather brogues appeared, followed by sharply pleated trousers. Bonnie didn't need to see the rest of the ensemble to know it was Uncle Jim. She reached for the teapot and put the kettle on the hob.

"Without denigrating your own personal tastes, I'm afraid Bonnie is correct. Your gifting is not sartorial." Jim said as he reached the last few steps. "Is that tea, Bonbon?"

Bonnie smiled, Jim's hearing was as sharp as ever. "Earl Grey?"

"Delightful." Jim's own expression was distant., distracted. He was already anticipating the reason he'd come. "When it's ready, perhaps we can retire to other quarters? I have something sensitive to discuss."

10

This wasn't his usual job. His gift was in charming his way into a situation and walking out with what wasn't his. He was always invited in, but he sought safety in numbers. If something went missing at an event attended by dozens of guests, Asher wasn't the obvious culprit. Tonight, he would be the only one there.

Asher felt underprepared. Fitz had given him no equipment, except for the microphone bug that he was to plant in the home office. He was told that he'd know where to put it when he got there, but how?

Steeling himself. He rang the doorbell and painted on a smile. Gloria, the housekeeper, answered. He would follow the script, act adorable and get what he wanted. At least this time, he wouldn't need to smuggle anything out afterwards.

"Hi, Gloria!" He beamed. "Did Kieran say I was dropping by? I have some reports for him to look at."

He waved the cardboard folder in the air to emphasise his veracity. There were reports in there, but like everything Asher produced at work, he knew they wouldn't be read. Gloria stepped aside and let him in.

"Mr Reuter didn't say anything, I'm sure you can just put them on his desk. Do you want a cuppa? I was going to make one for myself." She said.

"I'd love one." Asher grinned. "Are the family out?"

"Church. One of the girls is performing with the choir." Gloria shrugged. "I forget which one."

He chuckled. "And how are you?"

This was the way to gain trust. Ask the mark about themselves, show interest and they'd immediately assume you had good intentions. Adding something vulnerable or self-deprecating added an element of humility and made the mark more likely to believe your cover. Of course, it helped that he'd met her before and by all accounts had made an excellent first impression.

She led him into the expansive kitchen and flipped the switch on the kettle. Gloria hadn't been lying, there was a mug ready on the side. She fetched another one for Asher, all the time chattering about her husbands prostate and her son's job on a cruise ship. Asher nodded at the relevant places, storing the information for further use. It never hurt to have the staff onside.

Tea made, they chatted some more. "What brings you out here? I thought you were a city boy."

"Visiting mum. She's in a home out this way." He explained. It wasn't exactly a lie, her residential home was nearby, but he visited her yesterday, as usual.

"Poor dear," Gloria said. Asher wasn't sure if she was referring to him or his mother. It didn't matter. Neither needed her pity.

Truth be told, his mother was the reason he was here. The reason he did any of this. When Fitz approached him after that poker game, the promise of money to support his mother drew him in. The adrenaline high after he pulled his first job confirmed his decision. Poker taught him how to read people, Galvin taught him how to use his charm against them. He used both of those lessons to relieve the socialite Tara Montegue of her £100,000 pink sapphire and diamond necklace. The lift was clumsy and he was sure his guilt shone from him like a beacon, but as soon and he walked away from that party, he knew he wanted more.

~ ~ ~

Camera disabled, Bonnie tucked the EMP cannon into her backpack and retrieved the magnet from her boot. It was powerful: a neodymium super magnet. Paranoia prevented her from storing it too close to the rest of her equipment. Its power demonstrated itself when she stuck it to the side of the keypad of the lock and heard the click of the interior mechanisms shifting towards it. She didn't need a combination, she simply turned the handle and let herself in.

At the back of the house, the kitchen window was open and two voices in conversation sounded from within. Bonnie ducked out of sight and scrambled to the centre of the house. The dormer window was above. She assessed her options. There was a trellis running up the length of the building that would likely hold her weight, but the disturbed ivy would reveal her covert entry. The cast-iron downpipe was firmly fitted and in good repair. It would get her over the height of the ground floor windows to where the rough stonework had plenty of places to grip.

She tightened the straps of the backpack against her shoulders and found her footing. The drain pipe held. Bonnie shinned up a few feet until she could use the lintel of the kitchen window to push herself higher. She was glad for the recent dry weather, negotiating wet brickwork without a safety rope would have been risky. The nearest first-floor window she encountered belonged to a large double bedroom. The master bedroom. Bonnie had assumed Kieran slept in a casket (or more likely, nestled comfortably in Galvin Anderson's rectum) and it was jarring to see an assortment of pillows resting on a damask bedspread instead. The next window along was open, so she worked her way towards it.

Her climbing shoes were light, if tacky, and she made little sound on the tiled floor, even less in the carpeted hall. The home office was locked.

She had been thirteen years old when a little padlock dropped out of her Christmas cracker and almost smashed her side plate. The keys had gone missing by the end of the meal so Uncle Jim showed her how to open it with a hair grip. On Boxing Day, he produced another padlock and demonstrated how to pick it with a tension wrench and a short hook. Then, he showed her how to bypass the lock by shimming it with a flat piece of metal. By the time she saw him again in the Easter holidays, she had made her own rudimentary lock picks. Uncle Jim gave her a real set for her sixteenth birthday.

While the Chubb and Yale families built their empires on either side of the Atlantic, the Fitzduncans were suffering the effects of having invested in the losing side of the American Revolutionary War. They had land, titles and no money. Pride and arrogance sustained them until, two generations later, one William Fitzduncan bailed them out. He demonstrated a rogue entrepreneurial streak and not only invented the Fitzduncan Lock Box but raised the capital to put it into production. Her great, great grandfather sold the company, and the family had been living on the interest ever since. Bonnie assumed her uncle's interest in lock picking had been related to

William's legacy; she belatedly discovered it was more to do with a tradition her great grandfather had started.

It took less than a minute to pick the lock. Bonnie closed the door behind her and got to work.

~ ~ ~

Before long, Asher's cup was empty and Gloria had exhausted her repertoire of family stories. He picked up the folder. "I should drop this on Kieran's desk, it the door open?"

Gloria frowned. "Mr Reuter usually keeps that room locked, only lets me clean it when he's in there. You'll have to slip the folder under the door, most likely."

"No problem," At least, Fitz had assured him there would be none. "If it's okay, I'll use the facilities while I'm there, it's a long drive home."

It was easier to explain his longer than usual absence up-front than to make excuses later. Gloria picked another biscuit from the plate on the table, waving it towards the stairs at the centre of the house.

"I've just cleaned the family bathroom, help yourself."

Asher felt a little guilty about abusing her hospitality like this. Like her, however, he had a job to do. He climbed the stairs and located the office. It was the only door on the landing without a plaque to announce its purpose. The girls' rooms, master bedroom and bathroom were all labelled with hand-painted ceramic. Mrs Reuter owned one of those paint your own pottery cafes. The fact that the office hadn't been given the same treatment made Asher wonder if Kieran's constant working had garnered some resentment at home. Growing up, he had felt the same about his own father's workaholism.

The door was open like Fitz said it would be, even though the housekeeper was sure it was locked. Asher pushed the door and almost dropped the report in fright. Perched on the windowsill, like a sinister Peter Pan, was the woman from the other night. He didn't call out or demand an explanation like he imagined he would if he saw her again. He wasn't calm or composed.

"Y- y- you?" He stammered.

She winked and nodded towards an empty frame on the wall. "I don't want to keep you. It looks like you have a job to do."

"What..."

"Do me a favour? Shut the window behind me?"

"Wait," he said, too late. She had already climbed out of the window.

He felt like an extra in Zorro, who was that masked woman? Why did she keep turning up on his jobs? Below the frame lay the tools he needed for his job. The ones Fitz assured him would be waiting for him. It was time for a serious talk with that man.

~ ~ ~

"Earl Grey?"

"Delightful. When it's ready, perhaps we can retire to other quarters? I have something sensitive to discuss."

Bonnie looked at Martin and Giulia, who both shrugged. Either they didn't know what Uncle Jim had to say or they were deferring the news to him. She wasn't sure which was worse. It was something serious, he wouldn't have requested a private audience for something trivial.

Tea brewed, Bonnie set everything on a tray and invited Jim to lead the way upstairs to the sitting room. As she followed, she heard the inquisitive whispers of Martin and Giuly behind her.

"Apologies for dropping in like this, Bonbon, but I'd prefer to do this in person."

"Am I fired?" She laughed nervously.

Jim chuckled, but his hands remained in his pockets, jangling keys and coins. Her grandfather had the same habit and it drove her grandmother mad. "Nothing like that, my dear."

"So, what?" She poured tea into two cups and waited for Jim to settle into an armchair.

"The other thief. Asher?"

"Yes?" All kinds of scenarios ran through her head. What had Uncle Jim heard? Had something happened to him? Panic began to coil around her limbs.

"He... Well... Asher works for me. He was at Ahmed's at my behest."

Her cup didn't smash, it was cushioned by the sheepskin rug. Hot tea splashed her ankles. Numb, she heard and felt nothing.

~ ~ ~

He placed the report on the desk, sure it was bound for the shredder or recycle bin, and tried to shake off the disappointment of knowing that his career was ultimately futile. He was here to do a different, more fulfilling job.

Asher pulled the microphone from his pocket and placed it inside the empty frame, aiming the recorder towards the desk where the telephone sat. Following Fitz's instructions, he unrolled the painting and took a moment to admire it. The man had an art specialist, he'd seen her work before; he was always impressed by her skill.

He peeled the first section of backing paper from an adhesive strip at the top of the painting, he carefully lined up the canvas and pressed the edges to stick it down. The rest followed easily as he continued to peel and stick in sections until it looked like an untouched artwork. Asher stuffed the backing paper into his pocket, reminding himself to dispose of it later and headed back down the stairs.

"Thanks, Gloria," he said. "The door was unlocked so I left it on his desk."

"No problem, Mr Anderson. Can I get you anything else?"

Asher flinched at the name. *Mr Anderson is my father.* "Nothing, thank you. I should get back to the city, I have an appointment to get to."

The job was done, he should be satisfied. He was en route to his date with Bonnie, he should feel excited. Instead, all he felt was unease.

<h1 style="text-align:center">11</h1>

It had been a long time since she'd felt this nervous about a date. It wasn't even technically a date, they were friends —colleagues— meeting for a drink. Nothing could happen tonight. Nobody had explained that to the Top Gun squadron of butterflies who were loop-the-looping in her stomach.

Her nerves were compounded by what had passed. They had effectively worked a job together, even if he didn't know it yet. Jim assured her he'd explain everything to Asher this week, that he'd make sure he knew Bonnie had been as clueless as Asher until the Reuter job. All she had to do was get through tonight and her guilty conscience would be assuaged.

The rooftop bar was quieter than usual so she exchanged pleasantries with the bartender, Sophie, and ordered a drink. A crisp cold night and the mist that settled over the horizon had driven patron indoors. People came here for the views, without them, the warmth of the indoor bar was more appealing. For Bonnie, the lure of the London skyline was too great, even on a night like this. Growing up, London had been an exotic place, where Grandpa went to work and Uncle Jim did business. She dreamed of living there one day, although never anticipated the circumstances that eventually brought her here.

He wasn't late, she had a headstart from Sevenoaks, the trains running faster than the roads. She even had time to rush home and change before heading here. With every minute that passed, though, the more tightly coiled she became. That was why, when he did arrive, she kissed him on the cheek. Relief.

The fact that they both lingered after the peck meant nothing.

Yeah, Bonnie, whatever you have to tell yourself.

Asher, for his part, didn't appear perturbed by her over-familiarity. He smiled sheepishly as he greeted her.

"What are you drinking?"

She looked down at the empty glass on the bar. The bourbon on the rocks she'd ordered when she first arrived. It was meant to last longer than it had. "Another of these, please."

While Asher ordered their drinks, Bonnie found a table in a quiet corner of the bar.

"Cheers," she said.

He clinked his glass to hers. "Salud."

Bonnie raised the glass to her lips and felt herself wince. Strain in her forearm twinged with the movement, the past week's exertions finally catching up with her. She put the glass on the table and rotated her wrist.

"You okay?"

She rubbed her arm. "Yeah, my instructor is a sadist, that's all."

"Sounds like mine." He laughed. "He runs boot camps in the park on Saturdays, I'm pretty sure I died twice yesterday."

"It must be in the job description. I'm sure he's happiest when I struggle."

Comparing notes on whose personal trainer was meanest, they giggled and guffawed their way through the drinks. Asher trained three days a week before work and once at the weekend. Bonnie was impressed, she knew the commitment that took. Dangling from ceilings and hanging off walls definitely kept her fit. Without Dhruv motivating her, though, she wouldn't be as fit as she was.

"Same again?" Asher got up, pointing at her glass.

She'd been so engrossed in the conversation, she hadn't noticed how fast she'd been drinking. Then she looked at the time. She hadn't been drinking quickly after all; instead, the time had slipped away in his effortless company. "I'll get these."

He held out his hand. "No, no. I invited you. The least I can do it buy the drinks."

At the bar, he said something that made the bartender laugh, his body language easy and open. Uncle Jim explained that Asher's skill was in making people like him. He was personable and charming. People trusted his likeability, he exploited that. That might turn some women off him, not Bonnie. Her job was to get away before anybody saw her, his was the same; he just hid in plain sight.

She was staring. He noticed and smiled at her, heedless to everything she knew. Asher put the drinks on the table and slid back into his seat, next to her.

"Thank you."

"De nada," he said with perfect pronunciation.

"So, Spanish? I assume the Diaz part of your name comes from your mother's side."

He nodded, a lock of hair bobbed in front of his forehead and she resisted the urge to curl it around her finger. "My grandparents are from Zaragoza, but they lived in London for decades. My mum and uncle speak Spanish, I learned so I could eavesdrop."

The self-depreciation seemed rehearsed, like he'd had to explain away his knowledge before. Her father insisted Bonnie and Henry learn French because *'it's the language of Scottish no-bility,'* and she resented the obligation. Now that she was older, she enjoyed the opportunities it allowed her but could still recall the battles she fought to resist it. Asher's pride in his language skills was visible, yet squashed.

"Was your mother born in Spain?"

"No. Mi tío sí, pero el abuelo era embajador aquí en el Reino Unido y mi madre nació en Londres."

There was a reason why Spanish was one of the Romance languages, and it had nothing to do with its Latin roots. Bonnie's head felt fuzzy and her cheeks warmed. It could have been the bourbon kicking in. It wasn't.

"I have no idea what you said, but it was wonderful."

He chuckled. "My grandparents are Spanish, but they lived here for a long time. Mum was born here."

"Oh." She bit her lip. "Usually, Latin helps me out with translations but I got lost in the words there."

"You speak Latin?"

"I was expensively educated. The dead languages are important to the upper classes." She couldn't keep the acidic note from her voice. Memories of school brought out the orange hues in her litmus paper.

Although his mouth smiled, a frown dominated the rest of his face. "You didn't enjoy school?"

"It wasn't bad. Honestly, I was happy there. The sourness is retrospective."

"Okay." The frown lingered, his brows pushed together, agitating those soft brown eyes.

Bonnie put her hand on his, an action that came all too easily. She forced herself to look him in the eyes, even though she was sure there was no way out once she was caught in their beam. His features mellowed. Worry lingered in his gaze.

"Asher..."

He stroked her cheek and tucked a stray curl behind her ear. When he spoke, his breath rippled through her hair.

"Promise me you'll talk about this sometime? I want to know everything about you."

Hypnotised by the resonance of his concern, she nodded. "I promise."

There was such an intensity in the way he looked at her — she was amazed he didn't already know her every secret. The depth of his stare reached her core and churned her conscience. If he could see everything, would he still be here?

She didn't consciously lean in. Until his eyelashes fluttered on her cheek, she hadn't realised how close she was to him. His lips brushed hers, tentatively at first. Then, more assuredly, he kissed her. Bonnie grabbed fistfuls of his shirt and pulled him closer, deepening the embrace, tasting the ginger and lime on his tongue mingle with the whiskey on hers.

The bell for last orders broke them apart, breathless and bashful. Asher smiled sheepishly. Bonnie untangled her fingers from his clothing, cringing at the wrinkles she left behind.

"Thank you," he said and looked over the river to where the silhouette of the London Eye was emerging from the mist. "For choosing such a beautiful setting for tonight. The view is stunning."

"It's nothing. Maybe you can choose the venue next time? Something tells me we'll do this again."

Her voice didn't sound like hers. It was lower, more sultry. It was the voice she used when she was playing a part, projecting confidence she didn't feel. The one she used when she...

Oh no.

His face transitioned from euphoric recognition to angry realisation in a moment. His eyes burned with a mingling of betrayal and disbelief and Bonnie knew before he spoke. He knew.

"It was you."

Was it too late to play dumb? Could she bluff her way out of this? No. She screwed her eyes shut, expecting an onslaught. She deserved one. He should shout at her, scream abuse, tell her how deceptive she had been.

He didn't.

When she opened her eyes, he was still staring at her, mouth open, disappointment written across his face. That was worse. *'I'm not angry, Bonnie, I'm disappointed'.*

"Asher, I can explain."

He didn't give her the chance. Asher turned on his heel and strode out of the bar. She didn't chase him, there was no point. Numbly, Bonnie pulled her phone from her bag and stared at it. She should call Jim, let him know what happened. Should warn him that Asher was angry. She couldn't bring herself to do it. Jim deserved Asher's ire.

Angry at herself, she leaned her forehead on the cool glass and watched the mist sink into the city's streets. Tears prickled in her eyes and she furiously blinked them away. Lucy was right, the job meant she'd always end up hurting the people she got close to. She was foolish for thinking it would be different with Asher.

Secrets and lies. It was practically her family motto. **Her family** curse.

12

Asher lost his concentration and with it, his place in the drill. Instead of trying to get back on track, he took to taking his frustrations out on the practice dummy. Pummeled with jabs and kicks, the thing just stood there, taking his beating and all it did was make Asher angrier. Angry at himself. Angry at her.

Bonnie.

Those quick blue eyes. They looked less intense without the thick black makeup surrounding them, but once he had context, he realised why they'd been so familiar when they met his across the conference table. That sense of deja vu was nothing more than recognition, not fate, not love at first sight. It embarrassed him to consider how idealistic he'd been. She wasn't his soul mate and she'd probably been laughing at him the whole time.

He should have called Fitz, warned him that the accomplice he hired for the Reuter job was the same woman who beat them to the diamond. He couldn't bring himself to, Asher didn't want to admit to anyone how far he'd been taken in by her.

"Hey, hey! What did Donnie ever do to you?" Dhru put himself between Asher and the punchbag, arms held up defensively.

"Donnie?"

"Donnie the Dummy. You think you can beat the shit out this guy when you don't even know his name? What's up, man?"

In spite of everything, Asher allowed himself a smile. He adjusted his glove and caught his breath. His pulse pounded in his ears.

"Have you ever gotten close to someone, only to find out they've been lying to you?"

"No," Dhru said, passing him a bottle of water. Asher pulled a face, he didn't believe Dhru. "Really. I know everything about my friends. Why?"

"I was on a date on Sunday night, which was going well. Then, I found out that she was keeping something from me. Something major."

"That sucks, man."

"Yup." It did suck. He had trusted her and she betrayed that.

"And you've been completely and totally honest with her? About everything in your life?"

"I mean... There are things I haven't told her yet."

"Okay, isn't that technically a lie? By omission, sure, but it kind of sounds like that's what she did, no? The things you haven't told her yet, are they more or less significant than the thing she didn't tell you?"

"The same, I guess."

"You've spoken to her since? Heard her side of things?"

Asher faltered; Dhru was being unnervingly insightful about his situation. Guilt crept under his skin. "I... I haven't spoken to her."

Dhru nodded slowly, knowingly. "Right. It's Wednesday, man. That's a long time to leave someone hanging."

Asher wanted to shout at his trainer. The judgement in his voice was needling, as if he thought he knew more about the situation than Asher did. How could Dhru understand what it was like? He trusted Bonnie and let her into parts of his life he didn't open up easily. She repaid him with secrets and lies. She wasn't the fun and feisty work friend he thought she was, she was a thief. Too mired in his own disappointment, he shoved down the niggling sense of hypocrisy that tried to take hold. Dhru's tone of scepticism was warranted, but Asher wasn't ready to accept it. Not yet.

He sighed. "Dhru, I know you're trying to help but right now, the only thing that's working is beating the crap out of Donnie."

"Then carry on," Dhru said, stepping aside.

"Thanks, mate."

Asher resumed his assault of the dummy. Releasing pent up frustration and anger through his fists and feet. He'd ache all day, but right now, it felt good. Dhru stood and watched, arms crossed over his chest, a smirk on his face. Asher was sure his technique was all over the place. He didn't care. When he had finally tired himself out, limbs screaming and heart thumping against his ribcage, Dhruv lifted the dummy and carried it to the store cupboard.

"Make sure you stretch before you shower," he said.

The best thing about dragging himself from bed so early for a private training session was the knowledge that he'd have the locker room and showers to himself afterwards. The first class didn't start for at least thirty minutes. He and Dhruv were the only two in the building. He could take his time.

Asher closed his eyes and let the shampoo rinse from his hair, over his face. He wished he could wash his exasperation away as simply. On Monday, he sent a message to his father, saying he was too busy to make the morning meeting. It was a poor excuse, they both knew he was never 'too busy' at work. He didn't want to face her. Wasn't sure how he'd react to her.

He pumped the shower gel into his hand and started to wash himself. The coconut fragrance blended with the citrus in his hair and stirred up a memory. Bonnie on top of him. She'd been so self-congratulatory about her win that she lost all dignity. He couldn't equate that lighthearted, inelegant moment to the woman who dropped from the skylight and, literally, swept him off his feet. That woman was calculating and polished. She had lifted the diamond so smoothly that he hadn't noticed. That woman was not Bonnie.

Except it was.

When Asher emerged from the locker room, hair wet and bag slung over his shoulder, he waved goodbye to Dhru. He dropped the mats he was laying out and approached Asher.

"Hey, man, I'm sorry. I feel like I had a go at you today," Dhru said. "Righteous indignation, you know. I can't help it sometimes."

"No, no, you were right. I should speak to her. I will speak to her. Soon. I promise." Asher wasn't sure how soon that would be, but he knew he deserved answers and she was the only one who could give them.

Dhru turned away, paused and turned back. "Dude, I know we don't really socialise outside of these four walls, but would you like to come to mine for dinner next Monday? My parents are visiting this weekend so I'll have a fridge full of curry by then. My mother thinks I'll starve to death without her bi-monthly stock ups. After they leave, I always invite some friends over to deal with the surplus."

"I'm not sure." Asher didn't feel much like socialising.

"Dude, come on. Good food, company. You look like you need some fun. They're a great crowd, I'm sure you'll fit in."

He did need some fun. "That sounds great, Dhru. I'll be there. "

"Dhru's smile was beatific. "Awesome. I'll text you my address. See you later."

Asher would hardly call his conversation with Dhru a 'pep talk', but he left the gym feeling more positive than when he entered. Maybe all those people who claimed exercise was good for mood were less smug than he first thought. Endorphins were actually effective. Of course, the meeting with his father could still ruin his day.

"Asher, come in. Take a seat." His father waved his hand towards the plush leather seats on one side of the room.

Galvin's office took up one half of the top floor of the office building. Windows on every side afforded him panoramic views of the city. On a clear day, you could see Wembley Stadium. Asher sat down, more self-conscious than ever. He had done nothing wrong, well, nothing new, but he felt under scrutiny here. Galvin took his time finishing the email he was writing as if to emphasise how valuable his time was, and how insignificant Asher was in comparison.

"I can come back?"

"No, no. I'm done." Galvin's eyes lingered on the screen, even as he moved away from the desk and sat opposite Asher. "How are you?"

"I'm fine, father." *Not that you really care.*

"Good, good. And the ball? Do you have a guest confirmed?"

"Yes, thanks. You could have asked all this in an email, you know? Is there a point to this meeting?"

"Oh, yes." Galvin smiled thinly. The effort of small talk with his son was more than he was used to. "Well, I wanted to talk to you about your succession plan. You know I plan to hand the company to you in time."

"I'm aware." He'd been given no choice in the matter. Asher had been trained for this position from childhood.

"Over the next few months, I'm going to involve you more in meetings. I expect you to attend." Galvin paused. A dig at Asher's absence on Monday. "You need to commit to learning this role completely."

"Fine." It wasn't. Asher didn't want this, he never had.

"First, I think we need to work on your public image. Your profile is... It's not befitting the heir of such a company. It's time for you to step out into the spotlight."

Asher stared back at Galvin in disbelief. Why now? "If you're sure."

"I am. I'd like you to work with Miss Duncan to develop a strategy to raise your impact on social media. She's already making a real impact on our public image, I'm sure she can do the same for you. Once you are seen in a more positive light, we can start making you more visible during events, too."

Asher wanted to object. Wanted to shout at Galvin and tell him he didn't want to inherit the company. He didn't care about hotels. He certainly didn't want to run a chain of them. The business bored him. He grew up in it, he knew it well and wanted something else —anything else— for his life. Instead, he stared blankly back at his father. The idea of working with Bonnie made his stomach lurch.

"A more positive light? What kind of light am I in now?"

There was a knock on the door. Galvin must have been expecting it, he got up and opened the door himself. Behind it, was Bonnie. Wearing a crisp white shirt and black waistcoat over tailored black trousers and shiny stilettos, she looked like the epitome of business. Her hair was drawn back into a high ponytail, pulling all the softness from her features.

She wore many masks.

"Mr Anderson," she said. Her smile was thin. "You wished to see me?"

Galvin ushered her in and invited her to sit next to Asher. "You're right on time. I was just discussing with Asher his need for an improved public profile."

"Ah, yes." She turned her attention to Asher. Bonnie looked him up and down, scrutinising him like it was their first meeting.

"Asher doesn't understand what his current public perception is, Miss Duncan. Perhaps you can enlighten him."

Of course." She smiled at Galvin before turning back to him. "Well, Asher. Right now, you're a spoiled socialite who was handed a cushy job in daddy's office."

"Ouch." He winced. Was that the public perception or her opinion? "Tell it like it is, please."

He noticed that both Bonnie and Galvin called him 'Asher', but referred to each other by their titles. Was it to infantilize him? Remind him of his place?

"Look, Asher, I'm sure there's more to you than meets the eye. Hobbies, other endeavours? Most people would love to know what you really get up to at those society parties you go to. It's about looking behind the scenes and finding what makes you relatable."

Asher had been hit in the chest with a basketball once, the sensation now was comparable. Winded, he stared at her. "You want to delve into my private life? No."

"Don't worry, your skeletons will stay safely locked away."

Galvin laughed. "I doubt Asher has any. He's always been very by the book."

Bonnie pressed her lips together and Asher spied a flash of amusement in her eyes. He suppressed a snigger. There was a brief and wonderful moment where they shared the joke and Asher forgot her betrayal. Then, she composed her features and looked back at Galvin.

"Obviously. He's clean-cut and well raised, we can use that to our advantage. Perhaps Asher could make an appointment with me to discuss this further? I'm afraid I have preparations for this Sunday to take care of right now."

"Please, don't let me hold you up. Thank you for your input, Miss Duncan." Galvin stood and shook Bonnie's hand firmly.

"And, Asher?" He sat up and gave her his attention. "You know where I stand. You have my contact details, it's up to you to use them."

It was clear that the ball was in his court, but he still wasn't ready to talk. He wasn't ready to forgive her. His conversation with Dhru taunted him. *"I... I haven't spoken to her." " It's Wednesday, man."*

He would speak to her. Not yet.

As the door closed behind Bonnie, Galvin gave Asher a satisfied grin.

"There's a lot you can learn from her, son."

13

"Macgregor, how goes the investigation?"

"Full of dead ends and frustration, thanks. We're no further ahead than the last time I spoke to you. We're treading water."

Since she and Rez last spoke, Fliss and Arif had trawled through lists of guests, caterers, events staff, DJs, valets, cleaners and bartenders to find a link to any of the theft cases on her desk. With no one common denominator, they were playing join the dots without any numbers to guide them.

"About that. I think I've found you a new crime scene." Rez sounded so pleased with himself, Fliss could imagine the light on his face as he spoke.

"Where?"

"It's a little outside your jurisdiction. Sevenoaks."

"That's miles away!"

"Roughly thirty. It'll take you an hour to get here, but I promise to make it worth your while. There's a painting you have to see."

Fliss faltered. Technically, this was Kent Police's case, not hers. She should wait for them to investigate then ask to see the file. Bureaucracy could take weeks and her request could be denied.

"Rez, I..." *Fuck it.* "It's better to live with remorse than regret, right? I'll be there as soon as I can."

"I'll keep the place warm for you."

Fliss put her phone in her pocket as she slipped her arms into the sleeves of her jacket. She grabbed her keys and waved to Arif.

"I have to get to Sevenoaks."

"Why?" He blinked.

"I'm not certain yet. Keep things ticking over here, please? I have my phone if you need me."

Before anyone else could see her or question her actions, she hurried out, setting up the directions on her phone as she unlocked the car. The app predicted heavy traffic, she'd be lucky to get there before dusk. It was the type of place with an after-school rush hour, too. Rez's one hour estimate was going to be off the mark by a long way.

As she drove, she distracted herself with thoughts of the case. The myriad of possibly related cases confused matters. There had to be a way to narrow them down. Only cat burglars in movies left calling cards, but it would certainly make life easier for the police if the real-life ones joined in. Her team needed to find commonality, besides expensive things being stolen. That was why she was pushing her way through the Blackwall Tunnel. With every new development, the chance of finding that common denominator increased.

Or grew less likely.

Parking on the street was for permit holders only, the places that weren't were time limited, and full. Fliss considered abandoning it on a double yellow, but this seemed like the kind of area that she'd come back to a strongly worded note and a demand to speak to the manager. Instead, she called Rez, who told her to drive up to the gates which opened as soon as she reached them. The U-shaped driveway was long by London standards, she'd been to enough mansions since joining the taskforce to know. Fliss parked behind a black Jaguar XF, noting the worn appearance of her own ancient Volkswagen. The company cars were better in insurance, clearly.

The grey-haired woman who opened the door was expecting her. Ready with her enquiries about the traffic on the way in, she chatted non-stop as she led Fliss upstairs to a small home office.

"Ah, Gloria, you don't have to keep running after me." Rez grinned.

The woman practically giggled at his attention. Was that what she was like with Rez? Maybe Arif had a point.

"Mrs Reuter had to pop out, I'm afraid, but she said her husband is on his way home. This is his office, nobody else comes in here."

"Gracias, Gloria." The old lady grinned and left the room. Rez turned to Fliss. "I'm glad you could join me."

"What was so urgent I had to leave the confines of the M25 to see?" Fliss asked. She smiled but she wasn't joking. London was her comfort zone and her jurisdiction, outside its limits, she felt powerless.

"This." Rez presented her with a painting, using a gesture to rival the best 1980s game show hostess. Fliss regarded it.

"It's a painting."

"And?"

"It's an oil painting. Of some flowers."

"The nuances of fine art are lost on you, aren't they?"

Fliss shrugged. "It's not my forte."

"Well, this, Inspector, is a highly respected piece of art. A Sophie Van de Berg oil on canvas. It sold for more than half a million last month."

"Okay," she said, waiting for the punchline. "That's something you could have explained over the phone."

"Indeed. What you can't discern over the phone, however, it the subtle differences between this and the original."

He handed her his phone. She studied the image of the painting on the screen, preparing herself for a real-life Spot-the-Difference puzzle. The digital version and the picture on the wall looked the same. "I don't know what I'm looking at."

"Top left corner."

Fliss held the phone close to her face and examined the area before she inspected the original. Not the original. "The ladybird."

Rez's face crinkled while he smiled. The look of pride he gave her made her stand taller. "Exactly!"

She stepped forward for a closer look. The ladybird in the corner was red with black spots, on the image of the original, it was orange. Fliss didn't know whether it was a result of fading over time or if the artist painted it that shade, but the difference was clear to see. If this was a forgery, it was expertly done. The painting was beautiful: the flowers looked like she could pluck them from the vase and sniff them.

"That smell?" Her thoughts triggered her reflexes, she inhaled deeply. "It's chemical-y."

"Oil paints take a long time to fully dry out, the smell can linger. Old paintings don't have that odour. Another reason why I asked you here."

"This is a fake?"

Rez nodded. "It is. Yet, the auction house authenticated it before the sale. Someone switched it recently."

Fliss frowned. Rez clearly believed this was related to the other robberies but, as far as she was concerned, it wasn't linked. "My thieves just steal. They've never replaced their loot with a replica."

"No. I'll admit it's not the same MO, but this was slick, and that does fit the profile."

Fliss wondered what might make a thief change their operations like this. Everything felt wrong: the location was out of London, the forgery was a new twist. If this was her thief, why had so much changed?

Voices downstairs carried up to the office. A male, Mr Reuter, she assumed was speaking in an irate stage-whisper to Gloria. He sounded angry at being pulled away from work and was blaming Gloria for it. As far as Fliss understood, it was Mrs Reuter who invited Rez in to appraise the painting, and Rez was the one who called her. Fliss hadn't met him and she already disliked him.

She couldn't listen to that man berate his housekeeper any more. Fliss stood at the top of the stairs and held up her warrant card. "Mr Reuter? I'm Detective Inspector Felicity Stewart. Perhaps you'd like to join me up here and I can explain the situation?"

He scowled but started to climb the stairs. Fliss didn't wait for him, she went back into the office where Rez gave her a conspiratorial wink.

"What is this?" Reuter blustered as he barged into the office.

"Mr Reuter, I'm Carl Perez, Brache & Debar. You requested a visit to extend your insurance cover."

Rez extended his hand and Reuter shook it stiffly, as insolent as Rez was courteous.

"Mr Perez called me when he noticed a disparity with your new painting," Fliss said. "I'm the head of the Organised Theft Taskforce, he felt this fell into my purview."

"Why?" Reuter spat, looking at Rez, not Fliss.

She carried on regardless. "This painting is a forgery, Mr Reuter. It's not the original you bought at auction."

His eyes widened while the rest of his face remained impassive. This was definitely news to him but he was determined not to show it. "No, it's not."

"Has anyone out of the ordinary been in your house recently? Have you noticed anything unusual around your home? Has your security system activated for seemingly no reason? Security cameras stopped working?"

At her last suggestion he swallowed loudly, his Adam's apple bobbed exaggeratedly. "No."

Fliss didn't believe him. He was hiding something.

"Mr Reuter," Rez said. "This is not the original Sophie Van de Berg you bought. My company can't insure it as such."

Reuter glared at him. "Fine. Don't insure it, whatever."

"Sir, you need to file a report so we can investigate this." Fliss was already rehearsing her explanation for her presence for the Kent Police officer that arrived.

"No! I don't want to file a report. I'm sure it's just a mix up with the auction house."

Rez scoffed. Fliss wished she could get away with that. The scorn in his tone was clear. "Are you suggesting they were selling a copy on the same day as the original and the two got switched? Really?

"Of course not. I mean, they must have authenticated it wrongly. It's not a problem. Honestly."

Reuter continued his insistence all the way to the front door. He slammed it shut behind them without even thanking them for coming or saying goodbye. Rez raised his eyebrows and caught Fliss's eye.

"Interesting man."

"Yes, quite," she said.

Fliss was used to being rushed out of people's homes. Police officers made the public nervous; they were only seen when you were the victim of a crime or accused of one, neither were happy occasions. This guy, however, was in such a hurry to get rid of her that it made her suspicious. A creeping sensation climbed her neck, the sign of her cop-instincts awakening. She planned to check his record once she was back at the station.

14

Sunday rolled around, and Asher was still hurting. He didn't call Bonnie. If he managed to avoid her during the ball, he might never have to speak to her again.

Bianca was the perfect date for these types of events. An old friend, her father was a high-ranking member of parliament so she was experienced in navigating events like these. The icy grey floor-length gown shone against her fair skin, blonde curls tumbled down her back. She was elegance personified. Asher held his arm out to her and she held his elbow, allowing him to escort her into the ballroom.

He noted the camera at the side of the entranceway, well hidden from most of the guests. It was partially concealed by the decoration of flowers that coiled around the pillar it was mounted on. Few people would see it there unless, like him, they were aware of its positioning. Apparently, some of Bonnie's criminal skills were transferrable to her day-job. She had already posted time-lapse footage of the events team's set up on Instagram and Facebook and comments were flooding in under the posts.

As if thinking about Bonnie had summoned her, he saw her on the other side of the banqueting tables, talking to Galvin. She looked his way for the briefest of moments before turning her attention back to his father, but it was too late for him, he was transfixed.

She was stunning. Her dress had a black strapless bodice and a full, floor-length skirt that flared out from her waist.

117

Dozens of layers of tulle started black at the waist, fading into deep blue through to light teal at the ankle. Dark, smokey eye makeup made her eyes stand out, even from across the room, and her hair was pulled up into a tousled Dutch braid, showing off her pale shoulders. The man with a protective hand on her hip wore a teal waistcoat with his tux to match her dress. Bonnie's body was turned towards his, even though her attention was on Galvin.

For a fleeting moment, Asher regretted that he wasn't the one on her arm.

Galvin put his watch back in his pocket and put his hands on Bonnie's shoulders, kissing each cheek twice before shaking her date's hand. In that brief interaction, Galvin demonstrated more affection towards Bonnie than he had to Asher all year so far. His father's admiration for Bonnie deepened the wounds for him. She dared to deceive everyone in his world and made them all love her while he stayed in the background.

"Bonnie?" Bianca squealed. "Is that really you?"

"Bibi, oh my god!" Bonnie's voice changed, it sounded plummier; less Maggie Smith as Jean Brodie, more Maggie Smith as Dowager Countess. "You're exquisite."

"Please, look at you, you're like a steampunk princess. I always envied your style."

"You know each other?" The man with Bonnie was also out of the loop.

"Sorry, how rude. Martin, this is Bianca Payton-Eastaughffe, and old, erm, friend, and Asher Anderson-Diaz, a colleague. Bibi, Asher, this is Martin Palmer, my date for this evening."

They all shook hands, greeting each other cordially. Asher tried to ignore her description of him as merely a 'colleague'. What else should she have said? 'This is Asher, we sort of dated until he discovered that I also moonlight as a thief. We're not talking now because he's a massive hypocrite.'

"What a funny coincidence," Martin said to Bianca. "How did you two meet?"

"We were eighteen, it was the summer before I went travelling and we met at some god-awful event or other. Do you even remember?" Bianca turned to Bonnie who shook her head. "I was with my father and Bonnie was with her uncle. Anyway, we snuck off and, uh, made our own entertainment." The blush that started on her chest spread until the roots of her hair glowed pink.

Bonnie was unabashed by the memory. "That was a lot of fun. Do you still have the handcuffs?" Bianca squeaked in answer. "Excuse me, I have to say hello to someone, I'll be right back."

She winked at Martin, imparting some secret message that he instantly understood.

"I'll be fine here," he assured her. "I can get to know Bianca better."

Asher excused himself, too, suddenly suspicious, he was determined to follow Bonnie. She was up to something and he didn't want trouble for his father. He was almost disappointed when she stopped to talk to Lisa Jackson, the head of events. Directly behind them, Kieran Reuter was browsing the seating plan. If Asher joined him, he should be able to eavesdrop.

"Asher, my boy, you look very dapper." Kieran greeted him, more chipper than usual.

"Likewise."

"It's nice to dress up like this every now and then. Are you here to check your table?" Asher nodded and pretended to check the chart. Kieran was listing the fellow occupants of his table that evening, but Asher had tuned him out to listen to Bonnie. She and Lisa were discussing the guestlist and deciding who they should tag in the posts from the evening. He was suddenly self-conscious. Was his suspicion of her ridiculous? She might be a thief by night, but this was her place of work, too, and she was doing her job. He was a fool. "... Anyway, I'm going to check in with your father, enjoy your night."

"Yes, uh, have a good night, Kieran."

He shook Asher's hand and left, bumping into Bonnie as he did.

"Pardon me," she said.

"No, that was my fault," Kieran insisted.

As Kieran departed, Asher met Bonnie's eyes which seemed to glitter with devilry. Asher chided himself. He was a thief. Bonnie must know that, yet she trusted him, he had to learn to do the same. Without knowing it, Dhru had hit the nail on the head; he withheld information from her as much as she had from him. He wanted to say something to her, wanted to let her explain. He needed to forgive her first. How much longer would he be angry?

Now alone, he searched for somebody else to speak to. Asher was glad when he saw Bianca and Martin crossing the room to join him. Bianca scanned the seating plan, running her red stiletto nails down the names until she found hers and Asher's.

"We're sitting at the same table!" She turned to Martin, beaming.

Oh, crap. Asher put in that request over a week ago, before the rooftop bar incident and forgot about it. He got what he wanted, and now he wouldn't be able to ignore her over dinner.

He forced a smile. "Great."

When Bonnie finished speaking with Lisa, she returned to Martin. He wrapped his arm around her shoulder. Asher saw him squeeze her arm. Instinctively, Asher moved closer to Bianca. Bonnie placed her hand on Martin's chest and something roared inside Asher's.

"Do you have our cloakroom ticket? I left something in my coat," Martin said.

Bonnie smiled and opened her clutch bag. She passed him the chit. "Dinner's in ten minutes."

Martin kissed her cheek lightly and, as he did so, Asher was sure he saw Bonnie slip something into his pocket. He felt an urge to follow Martin out to the reception area, but Bianca slipped her arm through his and tried to draw him into the conversation. She kept a tight grip on him as she and Bonnie caught up on the years since they last saw each other. It was interesting to see how Bonnie continually deflected questions about herself back on Bianca. Fortunately, Bianca was happy to talk about herself.

Suddenly, Bonnie's focus drifted across the hall. He followed her gaze to where Kieran Reuter was patting his pockets with a confused expression on his face. When he started to make his way towards the door, Bonnie grabbed Asher's wrist.

"You need to head off Reuter. Now."

Asher snatched his hand away. "I don't need to do anything."

Her nails dug into his arm and her voice dropped to a hiss. "Stop being so fucking sanctimonious and do it or I'll tell Fitz that you blew everybody's cover out of spite."

Asher's mind spun in place like the chain had come off his wheels. He hadn't spoken to Fitz since last Sunday, on his way back from Sevenoaks. What had changed since then? On autopilot, he intercepted Kieran before he reached the door.

"Ah, Kieran, I meant to ask if everything was okay at home? You were called away on Friday."

It stood out, Kieran never left work early. If anything, he stayed late, worked weekends and volunteered for every overseas trip that nobody else wanted to go to.

"Fine, fine. A misunderstanding, easily sorted," Kieran blustered.

"I'm glad. It's not like you to duck out early."

"Yes. Sorry, my boy, I appear to have misplaced my phone, I'm on a mission." Kieran made to push past him. Asher's mind went blank, Bonnie had blind-sighted him again. He struggled to think clearly.

"Have you tried the cloakroom?" Martin appeared at his shoulder, waving an iPhone. "Mine was in my jacket."

"Good shout," Kieran said and strode off towards the foyer.

"You okay, Asher? You look like you've seen a ghost." Martin grinned nonchalantly.

Asher put his hand on Martin's shoulder, in part to steady himself. "Do you work for Fitz, too?"

"Fitz? Oh, do you mean Jim? You really should let her explain that whole thing instead of storming off."

The Maitre'D announced dinner and Martin left to join Bonnie and Bianca at their table. Alone, Asher felt worse than before. First Dhru, now Martin. He didn't give her a chance to explain, he reacted. Try as he might, he just couldn't shake off the huff he'd been carrying around since that night. He blamed her. He was angry with her.

Dragging himself from his self-pity, he took his seat between Bianca and Bonnie. The serving staff moved between them, pouring wine into glasses and placing bread rolls onto side plates. Bianca had introduced herself to Gabi from PR and her boyfriend, and John and Kelly, the executive chef director and his wife, they were chatting animatedly about something.

Taking advantage of the comparative privacy of the moment to whisper. "What the fuck, Bonnie? You work for Fitz?"

She shrugged. "Work for? No."

"This isn't the time or place to discuss this," Martin said. "Too many pairs of ears."

"Fine," he conceded, glancing to where Bianca was still in conversation with Gabi and David. Bonnie watched him, scowling.

"Nice plus one, by the way. She's been fishing for a rich heir for ten years, I hope you'll be very happy together."

"Not that it's any of your business. She's uncomplicated, I like that about her. And at least she's a natural blonde." He was being petty; he didn't care.

"No, she's not. Trust me." Beside her, Martin coughed, concealing a laugh.

"Is there anyone at this table you haven't fucked?"

"Yes." She stared him in the eye, unblinking. "You."

He deserved that. He could see the hurt on Bonnie's face, and he still pushed further. Anger was controlling his actions. He bit back a response and attempted to play nice.

Kelly and John shook hands with Martin as Bonnie explained to him who everyone around the table was. She must have done her homework because she knew as much about Kelly as she did John. Most people would have stopped short at the executive chef, but Bonnie went on to explain that Kelly was also a chef in a top London restaurant, acknowledging her achievements, too.

Kelly glowed at the recognition, immediately warming to Bonnie. "So, how did you two meet?

"At university. She chased me across the quad and begged me to take my clothes off."

Bonnie chuckled. "That's the abridged version."

"So what's the whole story?" Bianca joined the conversation.

"It was my third year, my final project was a modernist study of body image, and Martin has a beautiful body." Bonnie paused and took a sip of wine, unperturbed by the intimacy of what she was discussing. "And I didn't chase him, I approached him in a relaxed manner."

"Then she asked me to take my clothes off."

"Not just you. Guilia, Lucy and that dude, um, let me think." Bonnie acted coy.

Martin laughed. "My husband. The real reason she chased me across the quad–"

"–Approached. Calmly."

"Was because her best friend had a crush on me and she wanted to introduce us."

"It worked. They've been an item since the photoshoot."

"You're not together, then?" Gabi asked, pointing between the two. The whole table was listening intently, enjoying the exchange between Bonnie and Martin. This was a practised performance. Asher felt a wave of relief wash over him, she wasn't with him.

"No, just good friends."

Kelly leaned forward, resting on elbows. "Does that mean you're single, Bonnie?"

"Why, do you know somebody?" Bonnie smiled.

"That's not an answer," Bianca teased.

Bonnie picked up her wine glass and took a drink, enjoying the dramatic moment. Asher held his breath, anticipating her response. She could expose him, and after the way he treated her, he wouldn't blame her.

"It's complicated," Bonnie said.

"How so?"

"I work a lot. It can be a strain on a relationship. My last one ended because I prioritised the wrong thing."

John scoffed. "Please. That's an excuse."

"If two chefs can make a marriage work, you can find someone who understands your passions," Kelly added.

"I'm sure there's someone out there who shares your work ethic and isn't completely up his own arse about it, Bon," Martin said, catching Asher's gaze.

He wasn't talking about Bonnie's ex, like the rest assumed. For starters, Asher knew her last relationship had been with a woman. Nodding along with the rest of them, he tried to steer the conversation away from Bonnie.

"David, I believe congratulations are in order. Gabi has been showing off her engagement ring, she loves it," Asher said, hiding his satisfaction when every pair of eyes moved away from Bonnie and Martin.

Gabi pouted. "Oh, no. Don't talk about the ring. I accidentally chipped it. Dave had to take it to a jeweller."

As everyone else around the table rushed to sympathise with Gabi and offer condolences for her damaged ring, Asher turned to Bonnie.

"There's a cavity inclusion near the upper girdle facet that will chip in no time."

From behind her wine glass, he saw a triumphant grin. At least he now understood how she knew so much about diamonds.

15

Taking Sophie home on Sunday didn't make her feel better. Neither did crying on Dhruv's sofa on Monday night. She held herself together through that meeting on Wednesday, only bursting into tears once the door closed behind her. Poor Andrew wasn't sure how to react, all he could do was to hand her tissues and assure her that her mascara hadn't run. It had.

She was glad to have Martin by her side tonight. The moral support was appreciated, both in handling Asher and doing the job in hand.

Honestly, Asher had no right to behave in such a wounded way when he had lied to her as much as she had to him. If anything, she expected him to empathise with her situation. Instead, she was forced to play at cordiality with him while he got to act the huffy child. He hadn't even spoken to Uncle Jim since Sunday.

He could keep acting churlishly, and she would get on with the job.

When Martin returned from his SIM cloning mission, he informed her that Reuter's key card wasn't in his coat pocket. She had already ascertained it wasn't on his person either, but his departmental calendar had him in the office early the next morning. There was one place left to check: his hotel room. With Asher behaving like a toddler with a grudge, the task had clearly fallen to her.

After the dessert plates were cleared away, Bonnie excused herself from the table, stating work reasons. It wasn't technically a lie.

The room allocations weren't hard to find. Jim simply set Giulia loose in the system for twenty minutes. She had already upgraded Bonnie and Martin to a suite and arranged for a bottle of champagne and a cheese platter to be sent to Asher's. Reuter's room number was waiting on a text message when Bonnie checked her phone. In the elevator to the twelfth floor, she replied with a kissy face emoji and stuffed her phone back into her clutch.

The room was at the end of the corridor, the door around the corner to allow the inhabitants the illusion of seclusion and privacy. She uncoiled her under-door tool; she'd been sure it was going to spring out of her tiny bag every time she'd opened it this evening. Only luck had prevented it. Bonnie was undisturbed as she slid the tool past the plush pile of the carpet and fed it upwards towards the door handle. After a couple of failed attempts, the loop at the end of the wire hit home. She drew the wire back and felt the handle give. The door swung open.

Reuter's pass card and keys were on the bedside table on the left side of the bed. His phone charger was already plugged in, awaiting his return. A box of paracetamol and bottle of water sat next to the bed. Type A. She expected nothing less. It took fewer than two minutes to copy the RFID card with Martin's duplicator and clone the credentials to a spare key fob. Five minutes after reaching the door, she was closing it behind her.

It was that easy.

The first time she stole something for Uncle Jim was a different matter. Her friends stood watch in the book shop and caused the diversion she needed to slip into the back office. It had been clumsy. Bonnie was sure the guilt was written on her face all the way home; it weighed on her for a week. Dhruv, Lucy and Giuly were high on adrenaline and getting away with it; they eventually brought her around to the fun side of burglary. She got her hands dirty while her friends cheered her on.

At least, that's what they thought. The reality was, they were accomplices, and Bonnie knew that the sentences for aiding and abetting burglary and handling stolen goods were custodial. These days, they all knew the risks. Back then, they were naive and reckless.

Bonnie had learned to be more careful, more aware of her surroundings. Even so, she had let her guard down. As she rounded the corner to the elevator bank, an unwelcome figure made her jump. Asher was waiting for her, arms folded, face scowling.

"What the fuck is your problem?" She held her hand to her chest to stop her heart from bursting through her ribcage.

"My problem? What are you doing up here?"

"I'm doing my fucking job, Asher. One of us has to."

Bonnie punched the down arrow, imagining it was Asher's nose. She turned her back on him, too angry to look at his face. He grabbed her arm, and she wrenched it away, twisting it from his grip like Dhruv taught her to. She fought the instinct to react further.

Asher must have realised his error because he held his hands up and took a step back. He hissed, "you work for Fitz, Bonnie. What the hell?"

"Yes, and?" Asher's lips moved, but no sound came. She continued. "This really isn't the place to discuss this."

"It's as good as any other time."

"Really? You could have called Uncle Jim or me any time this week. Why now?"

Asher stumbled backwards. "Uncle?"

"For god's sake, Asher. I told you my real name, was that not enough of a clue? Bonameah Fitzduncan." She emphasised the first four letters of her surname.

"Who are you?"

"I'm Bonnie. The girl you met at work who drinks too much coffee and hates taking notes during meetings. I play with my Grandmother's ring when I'm nervous, I'm obnoxious when I win at games and I never get enough sleep. My favourite colour is teal, I don't like the taste of chocolate, I work all the time, but when I have it, I spend my free time with my friends, I climb, I run and I take self-defence classes with my best friend. I'm the girl who fell for your soft brown eyes and stupid messy hair at first sight. I'm a Social Media Manager by day and, like you, a thief by night."

Asher's stance altered. His arms relaxed, the crease between his brows loosened. "Okay, but..."

"I'm also Lady Bonameah Margaret Fitzduncan, the daughter of the Honourable Malcolm Edward Fitzduncan Esquire, granddaughter of the late Lord James Malcolm Fitzduncan. After my grandfather died, uncle Jim inherited his land and title; Lord James William Fitzduncan took his seat in the House of Lords and passed the responsibilities of the other family business to me. After everything they did for me, I owed it to them to carry on their work."

Her great-grandfather had started the enterprise. As a child during the Great Depression, he saw poverty from the window and wondered why he wasn't affected. As an adult, he pushed against the unfairness that some people were born into money while others struggled their whole life. As a Lord, he heard about situations caused by greed: vulnerable people taken advantage of, rich people getting away with it. He decided to make a difference. Bonnie wondered how he'd feel to know his descendants were continuing his legacy. Would he be proud? Would he even want that life for them?

The lift arrived, the doors sprang open. She stepped inside, waiting for Asher. He paused, arms once more folded petulantly over his chest. Sighing, she stepped back out and let the lift return to the lobby.

"Is this a Princess Jasmine in the marketplace deal? You're spending time with the common people or something?"

She scoffed. "Says the heir to the multi-national company fortune. If you grow up with a governess and a trust find, you hardly count as 'common'."

"I don't have titles, my lady."

How ladylike would it be to slap him? Her grandparents would probably have cheered her on.

"It's honourary, it means nothing! It merely means I'm related to someone with stature."

"It means your family is important. You are, too."

The laugh that bubbled out was a strangled scream. "My family? Don't you listen? My family disowned me!"

"Why?" He whispered. Excuses rose to the surface, reasons to defer this tale for another day. Even the long-story-short version was painful to tell. His fingers brushed hers, not brave enough to take her hand. "Tell me."

It was her most closely guarded skeleton in her closet. Her shame. Only a select few knew what happened.

Her secret.

No more.

No more secrets.

All they had done was tear her life apart.

Bonnie sighed and steeled herself. "I fell in love. Teenage, head over heels, stupid, obsessive love. Her name was Katie, and she was in the year above me. We used to sneak out of the dorms at night to be together. Nobody ever knew. She was the most important person to me, I thought I was the same to her. Until she left school to go to university and very publicly dumped me. My father decided I must be some kind of sexual deviant, even when I explained my sexuality. He doesn't believe bisexuality is real; he says it's an excuse for having loose morals. Basically, my behaviour was not befitting of someone of his reputation —he was the headmaster of the school— I should know better than to shame him. Suddenly, I wasn't his daughter anymore. He threw me out with just enough time to pack a small suitcase.

"That's when I came to London, using the cash I withdrew before my parents stopped my bank account. I knew there was one person who would accept me for who I was. My grandpa. When he died, my parents tried to stop his will. They thought I made him change it. I didn't want his money, I just wanted him back." Tears burned her eyes. She pressed her knuckles into her tear ducts, trying to suppress the flow. It was futile.

Asher shuffled his feet and examined his hands, refusing to meet her eye. "I'm sorry."

"I told myself that if I'd just kept it a secret, hidden who I was, my family would still love me. I'd still be a part of it, not some outcast who was cut out of all the photographs. I learned then that secrets protect you. Then, I learned that they don't."

He barked out a bitter laugh. "I should have stayed and let you explain. I should have trusted that you had good reasons for not talking about this stuff. You kept these things to yourself because telling them is painful. Instead of understanding, I took it personally. I was wrong."

The ball of tightly knotted fear she'd been carrying inside her for the past week unravelled. Not enough to forgive him, not entirely. It was a start. A strong start.

She sniffed. "Can we go back to the ball, please? Someone will notice if we're both gone for much longer."

He nodded and punched the call button. When the lift arrived, Asher pressed the button for the ground floor, Bonnie selected level 2. She'd get out there and take the stairs so they didn't return to the ballroom at the same time. She'd need a few minutes alone to compose herself. After a decade of building up a facade of strength, it felt strange to break down those walls. Strange, but secure. Somehow, in spite of everything, Bonnie felt safe in her vulnerability with him.

After fixing her eye makeup in the bathroom, Bonnie reached the ballroom to find the dancefloor full of people, Martin and Bianca included. The pair were dancing together, Martin spun Bianca, and she laughed playfully. Asher was watching from the sidelines. She stood next to him.

"Do you... Want to? I mean... Would you like to dance?" He asked.

"I don't know how..." She trailed off. She could dance, that wasn't the issue. She didn't know how to dance with him and not show everyone around that she was falling for him.

"It's Walking On Sunshine, not the tango. You'll be fine." He took her hand and led her into the middle of the crowd.

As soon as they turned to face each other, the music came to an end. The DJ leaned into the microphone. "Okay, ladies and gentlemen, we're going to slow it down and get close with Bob Dylan, Make You Feel My Love."

Galvin was a Dylan fan. Regardless, Bonnie made a mental note to throat punch the DJ later.

Asher looked more severe than she'd ever seen him as he stepped forward and slid his hand around her waist. Static electricity thrilled through her from where they touched. She placed her hand on his shoulder and grasped the other, inter-linking their fingers and praying that her palms weren't too sweaty. He pulled her in close. Something warm glowed in the pit of her stomach and spread to her chest. She felt dizzy. The beat of the music was like a heartbeat, but she knew her own was going much faster, more erratically.

The rest of the room melted into shadow. Only Asher was in focus. She rested her head on his shoulder as they moved in synch, her feet followed his without guidance. His hand on her waist directed them and her body followed his commands. The warmth inside her squirmed, she felt herself move closer still. Her head tilted upwards towards his, their lips inexorably drawn to each other.

"I hate to be That Guy, but can I cut in?" Martin tapped her shoulder. Bonnie's eyes snapped open, she couldn't remember closing them.

Asher jumped back as though he'd been electrocuted. "Oh, yeah, of course."

Martin took Bonnie's hand and led her away from where she and Asher had danced. He slipped his hands around her waist, and she wrapped hers around his shoulders, reminding herself that strangling him so publicly was a bad idea.

"Careful, Bonnie. It looked a lot like you were about to kiss the guy," he whispered into her ear.

Her face burned. She let her guard down in the worst place possible. What was wrong with her?

"Sorry, I forgot myself."

Martin laughed. "Girl, kiss whoever you like, just don't blow the job before we've seen it through. Did you copy the card?"

Bonnie nodded. It felt like a week had passed since she'd been in Reuter's room, yet it was less than an hour ago that she had excused herself from the table. In the fortnight since she started this job, much had happened. They were almost ready. There was one obstacle left.

"Do you think he'll be on board?" She asked Martin.

He shrugged. "I'm no expert, but if anyone can convince him, it's you."

16

Bianca wasn't staying the night. She was tipsy, and Asher offered her the bed to herself, but she insisted on going home. He made sure she was safely in a taxi, passing the driver his card to ensure the fare was billed to the company and thanked her for her companionship.

"It's probably not my business," she slurred. "But I think you like Bonbon, and I know she likes you too. She's sweet, you should ask her out."

"Thanks, but it's not as simple as that."

"Pffft! That's an excuse!"

"Okay, thanks for coming." He slammed the door and watched as the cab drove away from the hotel, losing sight of it after the first set of traffic lights.

Bianca didn't know the whole story. It wasn't that simple.

Yet, he had almost kissed Bonnie.

He started the night so angry at her, so determined to never forgive her. The truth weakened his resolve until he was back in her embrace. Like last Sunday, the world around him had blurred into bokeh, like in anime. All he could see was her. When Martin cut in, Asher had completely forgotten himself.

There was an ice bucket on the table, a bottle of champagne chilling inside. Next to it, a plate full of cheese and fruit. The note on the card read, 'The job hasn't changed. Neither has she. Fitz'. He stared at it for a full minute before making a decision. Asher grabbed the room phone and called reception.

"Hi, it's Asher Anderson-Diaz here, can I just check that Miss Duncan and her partner got a room okay? She was a late addition to the guest list."

"Mr Anderson-Diaz, of course. Let me check. Yes. She is in room 809, there are no issues whatsoever."

"Excellent, thanks."

He picked up the bottle and left his room, ensuring the key card was safely in his pocket. Climbing the stairs, he wondered what he was doing. What would he say? Would Martin be there? The questions tumbled around in his head until he reached the door. He knocked.

Martin answered, still wearing his dress trousers and shirt, the bowtie was gone and the top buttons were undone. Immediately, Asher felt uncomfortable in his tuxedo.

"Can I come in?" He held up the champagne. "I brought a peace offering."

Martin smiled slyly and stepped aside. "She's in the lounge."

Asher waited for Martin to close the door and followed him through to a spacious seating area. They had a suite! Was it the only room left or had there been shenanigans behind the scenes? He thought about the note from Fitz, the gift he'd arranged and opted for the latter.

Bonnie was sitting at a low table with several devices in front of her. Key fobs, SIM cards and a mobile phone were distinguishable among the detritus. She looked up with her eyes narrowed.

"Sorry, I couldn't sleep," he lied. He clearly hadn't been to bed, he was fully dressed.

"Okay."

"I'm going to pour a drink, you want one?" Martin asked.

"Uh, yeah, please. Whatever you're having." He handed over the bottle, and Martin took it into a kitchen area. He heard the fridge door squeak but no cork pop. They weren't celebrating. "What are you doing?"

"Working," Bonnie said. "I needed Martin to help me get this phone set up, tech stuff is not my forte. We're going to copy the RFID tags while I have the cloning machine on me."

He nodded, not understanding much of what she said, realising how much he still had to learn. "Sorry I wasn't more useful tonight. I was taken by surprise."

"I get it. Jim's need-to-know criteria is strict." She didn't mention his week-long sulk, which he appreciated. The phone lit up and triumph flashed across her features. "You must have questions."

She was all business again, almost as though their moment on the dancefloor hadn't happened. He sunk into the nearest armchair and sighed. He did have questions, but where to start? As he was considering that, Martin returned with three matching glasses, each half full of amber liquid and ice. He handed one to Asher before placing the other two on the table.

"It's bourbon. Never tell Jim we drank this," Martin said, laughing.

He gathered up the items on the table and packed them into a backpack with a laptop and a host of colourful wires. The pair spoke quietly as he did so, and Asher felt distinctly out of the loop. He swirled his drink and listened to the ice tinkle.

"Seriously, though. If Uncle Jim ever knew I drank whiskey with an 'e', he'd disown me, too," Bonnie said, reaching for her glass.

"Do you all call him Jim?" Asher asked.

"Pretty much. Most of the guys knew him well before they became a crew so it would have been weird to start calling him something different." Martin zipped up the rucksack and set it on a spare seat. He flopped next to Bonnie, who bounced a little with the force.

"Most of his associates call him Fitz, though," Bonnie said. "His poker buddies in particular."

"Oh, okay."

"Is that all you want to know?" Martin asked.

"Uh, no. I guess, why Reuter? Why here?"

"Opportunity. He refuses to meet with me so I can't steal his data like I have all the other execs." Bonnie curled her feet underneath her and leaned back into the chair. "He doesn't let his guard down at work."

That was why Fitz had him break into Reuter's home to plant the bug. He was more likely to be frank there than at the office. That thought raised another question.

"Why did we both have to be at the job at Reuter's house? I could have planted the bug alone."

Martin smiled, saying, "we know. You do all the jobs alone–"

"–That you know of," Bonnie said.

"This time, Jim wanted you to know you were part of a team."

"Besides, you couldn't carry the painting out the front door without raising questions. We need that," Bonnie interjected.

"Oh." All this time, Asher believed he was a lone operator. Now, Martin and Bonnie were suggesting otherwise.

He knew Fitz had a team, he'd even met one of them. The woman, Lulu, appraised gemstones for him sometimes. There was a hacker, too, and Asher wondered if that was Martin. Or was he the gadget man? How many others were there?

"It's a lot to take in," Bonnie said. "When Jim told me about your part in this, I poured Earl Grey on my foot."

"Which is the most serious reaction, in fancy circles," Martin chuckled.

Asher considered that. If Fitz really was a Lord, if Bonnie really had noble lineage, why were they stealing from their peers? "I still don't understand. How did you even get into this?"

Bonnie gulped the rest of her bourbon and put the glass on the table. "Uncle Jim taught me how to pick locks, I thought it was just a hobby until grandpa passed away, that's when Jim explained the whole enterprise to me. Turns out, I'd been training for this life without knowing it. I was a gymnast and ballet dancer; fencing was mandatory in secondary school. It made me light on my feet and gave me excellent balance. My best friend taught me self defence and showed me how to climb. After that, I just had to learn how to plan a job properly. Jim showed me how to start from the end of the job and work my way forward."

"Exit plans A through Z," Asher said. He'd heard Fitz say it often enough.

Bonnie smiled in acknowledgement. "Exactly."

"I was a late entry to the crew," Martin explained. He had a protective arm across the back of Bonnie's chair.

"He knew what we did for a while beforehand, though. I was still climbing in through downstairs windows or climbing up trellises when Martin came up with a better way to do it." She turned to Martin. "That was when you joined in an official capacity."

"Then the gadgets kept coming," Martin said. "Bonnie and I would spend nights talking about how she cracks safes and picks locks, and I would try to come up with ways to automate the processes."

"Some things are best done the old fashioned way. For the rest, Martin has made me a hundred times more efficient."

Asher wanted to speak, needed to recognise the trust they had shown in sharing with him. He couldn't find the words. Instead, he sipped his bourbon. It was sweeter than the whisky Fitz served him; Asher thought he preferred the Scotch stuff.

"It's late, I'm going to get some sleep." Martin kissed Bonnie on the top of her head and waved stiffly to Asher before leaving the room. The door made a scuffing sound on the thick carpet as he pulled it shut behind him.

Words continued to betray Asher. Jumbled thoughts interrupted each other. Nothing coherent came to mind.

Bonnie spoke. "I didn't sleep with Bianca, for what it's worth."

He blinked. Bonnie's history with Bianca was amongst the questions that were tumbling around in his head, but it wasn't at the forefront. "Uh, okay."

"I let you think that because, well, I wanted to get one up on you. I'm an ungracious loser. The real story is that I taught her how to pick the lock on her father's bureau. He used to confiscate her phone; she wanted to be able to get it back. I also showed her how to get out of handcuffs. I don't know if that was a party trick or if there was any real-world application, I never asked."

"Thanks. For telling me, I mean."

"We're telling the truth here, I figure it should be the whole truth." She shrugged. "So, how did Jim get you roped into this?"

"He asked me." There was no family loyalty to play on, no coercion required. Fitz offered him adventure and excitement, and Asher took the chance with both hands.

"That's it?" Bonnie's eyes widened.

"Yeah. I was recently back from America and bored. Fitz said the money would help with my mum's care, but I would have done it regardless."

Fitz had seen something in Asher that made him useful. His ability to read people was only part of it; his place on the guest list of most socialite parties was more significant. Asher had long used charm to make people do what he wanted, working for Fitz strengthened that skill. Sometimes, if the job required it, he took it further and seduced them.

The job had required it in the past, and would again. Could he do that to Bonnie?

He stood up abruptly. "I should go."

"Why?" Bonnie got to her feet, too.

"This job. I do whatever it takes to get my prize. It's not fair to expect someone else to share that burden."

Bonnie's laugh was dry and humourless. "Really? Of all the people you could use that excuse with, you're trying it with me? This job is my life. If there's anyone who understands your burden, you're looking at her."

He didn't want to cry in front of her, but his heart was rending in two. She was right. He still couldn't betray her like that. "I've slept with women to steal from them."

"Same. And men. What's your point?"

Prickles of envy crept over him, tensing his shoulders and balling his fists. He hadn't considered that. Every fibre in him was warning him that a relationship with Bonnie would be hard work. Asher would have to face more than just his father's disapproval, but his own ideas of trust and respect.

"I..." He took a deep breath and calmed his racing thoughts. "Since the night at Ahmed's, I haven't been able to stop thinking about the woman in black who swooped in and saved me from being caught by security. Only one person could get her out of my mind: you. Finding out you were the same person was a massive mind-fuck. I'm still getting my head around it."

"I understand." She stepped back, folding her arms across herself.

"No, I don't think you do." Asher closed the gap and reached for her hand. It was cold. "I want you. Want to be with you. I just..."

"You need more time?" She suggested.

Asher nodded. "I'm sorry."

He turned to leave as his gut cried out at him to stay.

Bonnie touched his arm. "Wait."

He shook his head, not trusting himself to say any more. Before she could change his mind, he closed the door between them. Immediately, he regretted his decision.

17

Dhru's home was in a quaint cul de sac, just behind the high street. Well-tended flower beds and neat lawns lined the road, it was the sort of area where you could forget you were in London. Asher double-checked the house number before he stepped onto a path that led to a red front door with ivy trailing around and up towards the recently painted eaves. He had to surmise that the exterior decor was Dhru's husband's domain: his personal trainer had never once indicated an interest in anything like this. When Dhru answered the door, Asher reconsidered his assumption. Virtually unrecognisable in smart jeans and a white t-shirt under a wheat-coloured blazer, Dhru welcomed him in, ushering Asher through to the immaculate kitchen. There was more to Dhru than crunches and timed laps around the park.

Throwing that thought into even more stark relief, Dhru introduced him to his husband, Martin. "I believe you've met before?" he asked.

Asher gawped. He tried for words, but none obliged him so he continued to open and close his mouth, hoping sounds would ultimately form. They did not.

"Surprised?" Dhru asked.

Martin chuckled and opened a bottle of beer, passing it to Asher. "If it helps, I've been in your shoes. When I met Dhruv and Bonnie, they'd been doing the criminal pastime thing for two years. It was a lot to take in."

"Uh," Asher managed. He took a swig of beer and tried again. "When did they tell you?"

"About six months into our relationship." Martin looked to Dhru for confirmation. "Once he was sure he could trust me."

Six months... *Once he was sure he could trust me.*

Shit. He had reacted without thinking, kept secrets from Bonnie while punishing her for doing the same. She couldn't trust him. Not yet. He hadn't earned it, especially not this past week. "I've been an idiot, haven't I?"

Dhru clinked his bottle against Asher's. "Yup."

Asher was still reeling over the new information when the doorbell sounded. That was when it hit him: Bonnie was likely an invited guest, too. He gripped the beer bottle so tightly, he was sure it would shatter. He needn't have worried. The recent arrival was a pretty woman, all dark curls and smiles, who introduced herself as Giulia. She was followed closely by Lucy, a vaguely familiar redhead in paint-splattered jeans.

Giulia handed him a bowl of snacks, smiling kindly as Martin insisted they take a seat in the adjoining sitting room. Asher perched on the edge of the sofa, still trying to shrug off the feeling of being ambushed. Meanwhile, Lucy scrolled through the playlists on the huge flatscreen television, critiquing Dhru and Martin's tastes.

"I'm sure you'll find some Indigo Girls if you search hard enough," Dhru quipped.

Giulia sat on the cushion next to Asher and curled her feet under her. She regarded him with interest. "As one of the best friends, I think I'm meant to threaten you with bodily pain if you hurt Bonnie, but I'm not a fan of violence. I can doxx you, though. Expose every single one of your secrets."

"Besides, she's been learning Wing Chun with me since 2008. I'm sure Bonnie could hurt you herself if she needs to," Dhru added, smirking. The buzzer sounded again. "Speak of the devil."

In the kitchen, Martin put his finger to his lips and nodded towards the hallway. The others fell silent, grinning in anticipation.

"Bon! I said, bring drinks! What is all this?"

"I did bring drinks!" Asher heard glass bottles clicking. "What do you think? I told Auntyji I was coming for dinner tonight and she said, 'beta, there won't be enough for everyone, bring chapati.'"

"Why were you talking to my mum?"

"She called yesterday. "What was I meant to do?"

"You didn't have to bring extra food, you know mum is an overcaterer. Bon, this is way more than just chapati." The group giggled at Dhru's exasperation. This was clearly a regular occurrence.

"Look, if she tells me to do something, I'm not going to disobey. Would you?"

Resigned silence followed. Dhru's mother was obviously a force to be reckoned with if neither Bonnie nor Dhru were willing to stand up to her.

"What else did you bring?"

"Just samosa and bhujia."

"And?"

"Halawa."

"Why?" Dhru cried exaggeratedly.

In the living room, everyone dissolved into peals of laughter. Everyone, except Asher. Martin leaned over and whispered conspiratorially. "She turned up at university with no family. Dhruv's parents kind of adopted her. Those two are like big brother and little sister."

"Mine, too," Giulia said. "Whenever Sylvie and Matteo visit London, they bring as many gifts for her as they do for me."

Bonnie was still bickering with Dhru as she walked into the kitchen, so it took her a split second to notice him. "Oh, you absolute bastards!"

"Did we not mention Asher was coming tonight?" Dhru asked in the least contrite tone Asher had heard. "Oops."

If looks could kill, Dhru would have burst into flames on the spot. Bonnie was furious in a dangerous, simmering way, Asher was glad he wasn't Dhru right then. She appeared to be ignoring him, which suited him fine. Her ire was directed solely at Dhru. Martin gave them both a 'not in front of the children' glare.

"Okay, you know you can't stay mad at Dhruv for long so why don't you help me serve the food, Bon," Martin said, then turned to Dhruv. "You, freshen up the drinks."

Asher was quietly impressed. In his family, if someone had pulled a trick like that, the huffy fallout would have lasted a decade, minimum. The Anderson family motto was, 'We Bear a Grudge'. Apparently, all it took for Bonnie and Dhru to make up was a cold beer bottle on the back of the neck and a retaliatory tea-towel whipping.

She looked good. Bright-eyed and laughing with Dhru and Martin, this was clearly her comfort zone. Her demeanour was more relaxed than he'd seen her since that night at his flat. Her grey sweatshirt slid off her shoulders and she didn't feel conscious enough to pull it up. She had no hang-ups with these people. He had always thought she was beautiful, but here, she was breathtaking.

"We've met, haven't we?" Lucy said, perching on the arm of the sofa.

Asher nodded, squinting at her. "I'm sure we have, but I can't place you."

As tall as he was, she commanded an intimidating presence. There was a calm control in her demeanour that made him sit up straight and pay attention. There was an office tower full of management wannabes that would have killed for charisma like hers.

"I thought the context might jog your memory." She waved her hand towards the others. He saw her in profile and remembered.

"Fitz? Oh! You were there! When I did my first job."

Lucy grinned. "You were an arrogant little shit back then."

Asher shrugged. It was true. "I was proud of myself. I didn't think I'd be able to do what I did." Lucy nodded, smirking. "And, yeah, I was arrogant as fuck."

Across the room, Dhruv and Bonnie were jousting with wooden spoons. He wasn't sure if he'd ever seen the lightness in her expression before — she shone with beauty.

"I'm the ex-girlfriend. I wasn't sure if she said." Lucy followed his line of sight. Asher muttered an acknowledgement; Bonnie had mentioned an ex-girlfriend, but he never thought their paths would cross. He wasn't sure how to respond. "Look, I know the others have given you the hurt-her-and-I-hurt-you routine. I'm not going to pile on. I will say, though, she's been let down by a lot of people in her life, don't be another one."

"I'm afraid I already have. I plan to redeem myself as often as possible."

At that, Lucy smiled for the first time that night and tapped her bottle against his. "That's all I ask."

They drank together in comfortable silence while Bonnie and Dhru squealed and chased each other around the kitchen and Martin tried in vain to make them cooperate in serving dinner. In the end, they compromised by setting the dishes out on the island unit and encouraging everyone to come and help themselves.

While they ate, Asher tried to survey the dynamic between the friends. Dhru and Bonnie were like brother and sister, all light-hearted squabbling, competitiveness and unconditional affection. Martin was more sedate, more sensible; he was protective and playful. Asher didn't like the term 'mum-friend', but it described Giulia better than anything he could coin himself. She was the one who drew Asher into the conversation whenever he started to feel like he was on the periphery.

As Bonnie gathered the empty plates and passed them to Lucy, who loaded the dishwasher, Dhru stretched out, groaning. They had all made a valiant attempt to consume the curry, but the sheer quantity had won in the end. Asher was ready for a nap.

Martin yawned, similarly succumbing to the soporific effects of Too Much Food.

"I need sugar. What's for dessert?"

Giulia's mouth twitched as she went to the fridge and removed a pastry case topped with towering meringue. Pink filling leaked out around the sides.

"Is that?" Lucy leaned over to get a better look.

"Giuly, your desserts are amazing, but the puns have to stop," Bonnie said.

"I beg to differ. Puns make everything better." Giulia placed it in the middle of the table and brandished a cake slice. "Who's first?"

Asher didn't get the joke. "What is it?"

"Raspberry pie," all five said in unison.

"I don't get it."

"Wow, you really do just turn up places and act adorable, don't you?" Dhru shook his head. "I thought Martin was exaggerating."

Giulia served the pie. For all that the others thought it was some kind of joke, it was delicious. They chewed in satisfied contemplation for a few minutes until Martin carefully set his fork on his plate and looked at Asher with interest.

"Do you really not know what raspberry pi is? What about a Pineapple? Rubber Duckie? Tell me you use a VPN?"

"Martin, he still phones in his takeaway orders. He's a lost cause." Bonnie said, her eyes almost caught Asher's until they flicked away at the last second.

Asher wanted to defend himself, but he didn't know what the things Martin said meant.

"Oh, honey, you and I need to make a date after tonight. Someone has to introduce you to the present day." Giulia patted his shoulder patronisingly. He just nodded.

Changing the subject, he asked. "So, I know why Bonnie does this, but what about the rest of you? If you don't mind me asking."

Dhru, Giulia and Lucy looked at each other, grinning. Without words, Lucy was nominated as the spokesperson.

"Proximity, mostly. We were friends when Jim asked Bonnie to do her first job. She needed help and we did it without fully considering the legality. By the time we thought about the laws we'd broken, we were in too deep and having too much fun to give up."

"There was a situation. Someone died and left a valuable asset to the person who'd been there for him in his last days. The rest of the family objected and tried to prevent the will from being executed. It was ugly and caused a lot of heartbreak. It was… " Dhru trailed off, unable to articulate.

Asher knew they were referring to the incident with Bonnie's parents after her grandfather's death. The friends didn't know that he was aware of the whole story.

Giulia reached out and took Bonnie's hand in both of her own. "We saw how Jim stepped in and smoothed out the drama. He was ferocious, it was awe-inspiring to watch. When a similar situation arose a few months later, and we were able to help, we jumped at the chance. It was like paying it forward."

Lucy continued. "Bonnie was the one with the skills to do the job. We provided the distractions and watched for anyone who might get in the way. It's what we still do for her. We're better at it now, more sophisticated, but our role is the same."

"It's more than that," Bonnie insisted. "You give me the tools I need to do the job. I do the easy, grabby bit. You guys do the clever stuff."

In spite of the copious volume of food in his belly, Asher suddenly felt empty. The camaraderie, support and unquestioning love these friends had for each other was enviable. He'd been isolated from his peers for most of his childhood. After his mother's breakdown, her family stepped in and offered to care for Asher. Pride and pettiness prevailed, and his father chose to keep him close instead. Behind his nose and throat, a lump formed, preparing to unleash tears. He sniffed and shook his head.

Perhaps noticing, Lucy leaned forward, elbows on her knees. "Should we get down to business?"

Bonnie nodded. "Let's."

"Asher? Do you know what the next job is?" Dhru spoke with the tone of someone with bad news.

"I'm guessing this is when we steal from Galvin?" He still hadn't spoken to Fitz, but it wasn't hard to deduce.

All eyes turned to Bonnie for the answer. She put her plate on the coffee table and dusted off her hands.

"It is." She looked directly at him for the first time that evening. "Do you know what we're taking?"

Asher shrugged. His father had many valuable items. One, however, jumped to mind. "The Coronation Watch?"

Bonnie blinked slowly before nodding. She was solemn, there was no schadenfreude. Not for her, at least. Asher was internally gleeful at the prospect.

"What is the Coronation Watch?" Martin asked.

Grinning, Bonnie leaned forward. "Are we all sitting comfortably? This is a story about a very important, very expensive watch. George the fourth was notoriously spendy, and what do you get the man who has literally everything? Well, when Caroline of Brunswick married him, she commissioned a Swiss watchmaker to create an extravagant pocket watch to mark the occasion. The story is that it was completed in the same year he became king, hence Coronation Watch."

"So, it belonged to a king? That's why it's special?" Dhru interrupted.

"Not totally. The watchmaker kept to his brief. He used gold and platinum wherever possible, and added rubies, emeralds and sapphires. The watch mechanisms contain the most intricate and cutting edge technology of the time. Honestly, it makes the Supercomplication look like a G-Shock."

"You're the only person in the room that gets that reference." Giulia grinned at Bonnie, who rolled her eyes. "Continue."

"Anyway... George died ten years later and his brother, who succeeded the throne, wasn't super fond of him, so he gave the watch away to the British Museum. It was there for centuries until someone stole it in 1970, and it was only recovered in the late eighties."

"Not guilty," Asher said. Martin and Dhru laughed.

Lucy asked, "so what does Galvin have to do with it?"

"Well, that's the thing. It was missing for seventeen years before it was anonymously returned to the museum. That's plenty of time to make a convincing copy, no?"

"Oh, shit." Asher was aware he'd spoken, but it wasn't his voice he heard. Both Lucy and Martin mirrored his sentiments. Bonnie looked like a Cheshire cat. She was enjoying this.

"According to Uncle Jim's information, Mr Anderson has the original Coronation Watch. The one in the archives of the British Museum is a forgery. That's not a thing you buy on eBay, or even Sotheby's: you've got to be very connected to some extremely shady people to get your hands on it. You also have to be crazy-levels of rich."

Five pairs of eyes settled on him, expecting an explanation. "My father collects antique watches, has done since he married my mum. It's how they met, my uncle sold him a few. There's a chest of drawers in the penthouse dedicated to them. I'm pretty sure he'd want to get his hands on one with a history like that. I have a good idea who might help him procure it, too."

"Someone who inexplicably still has a job in spite of the entire senior management team agreeing that his corner office is a waste of floor space?"

"That's the man."

"The dude we bugged?" Giulia asked.

"The very same. We know Reuter is the middle man between the black market and his wealthy friends. There's a likelihood he transports some of the items, too. His job involves international travel, it's the perfect cover."

"That's how he has the cash to buy Dutch Masters for his home office, I assume?" Lucy said.

"Oh, I'm sure his cut from the watch alone kept him in legitimate art and antiques for months," Bonnie agreed.

"Why? What's the watch worth?" Asher couldn't help himself.

"Its most recent valuation was thirty million."

"Pounds?"

"No, jelly beans, Asher. Yes, pounds."

"And we're going to steal it?" Dhru confirmed.

"Yes."

"How?" Asher asked. "My father is ultra-security-conscious."

"No wonder," Dhru coughed.

"Tell me all about his security measures, especially safes," Bonnie said.

"Yeah, Asher, talk dirty to her." Dhru earned himself a smack on the arm from Bonnie.

"At the office, he has an Alconbury 350 with dual custody locks and digital keypad access. The door to the area has a Soteria voice-activated smart lock that's set to respond to only him. At the penthouse, he uses the safe that came with the room, but that room is guarded twenty-four hours a day by reception staff, elevator attendants and a bodyguard. The doors have high-security locks, not keycards, and only dad and Candy have keys."

Lucy snorted at the name 'Candy' and Asher agreed with the sentiment. It wasn't her real name: the photographer at her first shoot apparently told her she was 'sweet like candy' and the name stuck. If true, Asher blamed everyone around her for not pointing out how queasy that story would make most people feel. Not his father. Galvin wasn't most people.

"Hotel safes are easy pickings, but I don't like our chances of getting in without detection. The office is an easier target, although the Alconbury is a tough one to crack." Bonnie sighed. "Two locks, nine pins in each, deep, awkward keyways that would need to be picked simultaneously to open the door."

Asher's anticipation fizzled. "That sounds impossible."

"You shouldn't have said that," Giulia hissed through her teeth.

"You poked the bear," Martin added, shaking his head.

Bonnie rolled her eyes at them. "I will not stoop to your level. Let's put the safe to one side for a moment and consider the rest. Giuly, can you access the security system?"

"Of course I can." She grinned. "I may already have done it."

"Good, I'll need you to disable the alarms and cameras. Martin, the keypad, can you deal with that?"

"I'm sure I can come up with something," Martin said.

"Dhruv, We need a rooftop getaway. Something that leaves minimal trace." Dhru just nodded. "Lucy, can you research the watch, please? Give us a rough sketch of what we're looking for?"

"On it."

"Okay." She turned to Asher with a terrifying glint in her eye. "That's plan A."

As soon as Bonnie left, Asher announced his own departure. He knew she'd walk to the nearest bus stop, so he jogged to catch up with her. As he rounded the corner, he saw her walking briskly ahead.

"Bonnie, wait!"

She turned, frowning. "What, Asher? I'm giving you time, what else do you want?"

"That plan, do really think it'll work?"

"I do. So long as we all stick to it, I'm sure we'll get everything we need. Why? Are you having second thoughts?"

Asher closed the gap between them and reached for her hand. "No. No second thoughts. I've, uh, actually gone back to my first thought. The one I had in the conference room when I first met you, in my flat when threw yourself at me..."

She giggled. "Not how that happened."

He shrugged. "… At the rooftop bar when you kissed me, and on the dancefloor when you held on to me like you might fall."

"What was that thought?" She whispered, tilting her chin towards him.

"That I want to take you home with me. I want you."

She looked up at him, eyes glassy and lips parted. He leaned towards her, the scent of her perfume in her hair drew him in. When their lips finally met, all the anticipation was worth it. It was more magical than his wildest imaginings. Her fingers coiled in the hair at the back of his neck and she pushed herself into his body, he instinctively held her tighter.

"Let's do this," she said, and took his hand.

18

DC Maamoud was still at his desk when Fliss finally switched off the lights and locked the door to her office. She approached him and noticed with a pang of guilt that he was still sifting through the list of credit card users who purchased the thief's combat boots from London boutiques.

"That can wait until the morning, Arif," She said. "Go home to your family, it's late. The DCI won't keep authorising the overtime unless we get results."

"That's what I'm trying to do. Get results." He waved his hand over the pile of papers in front of him. "I'm cross-referencing these receipts with anyone on our databases. So far, a known embezzler bought a pair, but he's been in prison for the last six months. Another pair was bought by a guy with a decades-old conviction for Public Intoxication."

Fliss sighed, this case was one frustrating dead-end after another. Every time they thought they had a promising lead, it sputtered out. She had been as hopeful as Arif that the boots would yield fruit, but so far, nothing. She knew that there was always the likelihood that the thief paid cash for hers, bought them second hand or received them as a gift. Whoever it was, male or female, they had gone to extreme measures to avoid detection. It seemed fair to assume they wouldn't leave a paper trail either.

"Do we have anything else? There must be another avenue to try," she said.

We could check payroll records for caterers and party planners at the events?" Arif suggested.

She nodded, unconvinced. They'd exhausted the guest lists and vendors. At this point, they were going in circles. "We can check those tomorrow. Come on, grab your things. I'll drive you home."

As he shut down his computer and tidied his desk, Fliss waited. Guilt renewed. Arif was more invested in this case than she was, each challenge they met drove him on, made him more stubbornly determined while she grew increasingly disheartened. He was young, this was his first job as a detective, she'd hate for him to become as demoralised as she was over it.

They plodded down to the basement, both weary from the day.

"If only there was a way to know which scenes were linked. We could be dealing with a team, two different operators or a single thief and we still don't know which," Arif said, sighing.

"I know. Without some kind of calling card or signature, I'm not full of optimism about that."

In the dimly lit parking structure, Arif stopped in his tracks, eyes wide and a grin on his face. Fliss could almost see the lightbulb illuminate above his head. He looked left and right, as though checking for evesdroppers.

"In most of the scenes we've gone to, there have been security system glitches, right? The footage is erased or the camera is somehow deactivated. What if the thief is hacking the networks?"

"It's very possible," she agreed. Fliss had considered it herself, but couldn't see how it would help to narrow the list of suspects.

"Let's ask the tech guys to look through the hacked systems. They might find the code they used to access them. I read somewhere that every hacker's code has individual elements that we might be able to identify. Like a signature." He paused, probably noticing the look of incomprehension on her face. "It might not help us catch the guy, but we'll get a better picture of which crime scenes they're actually responsible for."

"It sounds deeply complicated," Fliss said. "We're out of simple options, though, so let's try it. We'll contact the cybersecurity team in the morning and see what they come up with."

Not for the first time, Fliss's heart sped up, and goosebumps spread up her arms. The thrill of the chase wasn't gone, not totally. Each new lead, every path of enquiry opened up the possibility that, against all the odds, they might solve this case. She shivered even though the weather wasn't cold.

"There's a consultant I've worked with a few times, she's a genius with code. Do you think we can use the budget on her?" Arif asked.

"We can ask the bosses. Actually, I've been working on a list of possible targets based on that snippet Rez gave us, about the diamond not being completely kosher. People with suspected links to black market dealings who have expensive enough lawyers that they've never been charged with anything."

"Have you asked Rez for his input on that list? He must know more than we do there. He sees all sorts of suspicious items that we never will."

"Good point. I'll call him in the morning, too."

Arif smirked. "You could call him tonight. Maybe you'll graduate from a coffee date to dinner?"

Fliss started the engine and allowed herself a smile. "I'm pretty sure this counts as insubordination, Maamoud."

<h1 style="text-align:center">19</h1>

"Alright, Clueless, let's drag you into the twenty-first century." Giulia didn't wait for an invitation, she pushed past Asher and started setting out equipment on his dining table. He stood and watched helplessly; he wasn't used to having visitors to his flat, let alone ones who made themselves at home so easily. It was disconcerting.

"Uh, do you need anything?"

She looked up from where she was connecting wires into a box. "Yeah, if you're making coffee, I'll have one. Black, one sugar. And, show me where your router is, please?"

Asher pointed to the corner of the room where the television stood. Momentarily, he wondered if he should apologise for the mess of wires and cables behind the media unit; he didn't have the strength. He left Giulia to root around in the clutter while he set up the coffee machine.

He wasn't exactly computer illiterate, he used various systems at work to compile data and draw out statistics. He knew his way around Outlook and Excel, which was more than half of the senior management team did. The world of hacking and coding was beyond his understanding, though. It was something he'd never needed to use. There were guys at college, Computer Science grads he'd met at poker games, who could do impressive things with their battered laptops covered in stickers. They could predict hands of cards with alarming accuracy. Their algorithms were banned, however. Asher had all he needed to count cards in his head.

He put Giulia's mug of coffee on the table and sat opposite her, clutching his own. "What are you teaching me today?"

"Some basics. I'll set up your VPN." She smiled at his vacant expression. "Virtual Private Network. Every internet connection comes with a unique number, a code that tells people where you are and what network you're connected to. It can be hacked. A VPN will protect you from that."

"Oh, okay. Thanks."

"Apart from that, I have a fun little voice changer programme to show you."

That wasn't too overwhelming. Giulia and Martin certainly earned their places in the team if they had to do this for every job. Asher drank his coffee and thought about the security system at Prince Ahmed's, and how he thought he'd understood it. He'd been wrong.

"So, how do you get into a system like the one at HQ?"

"Easily. Bonnie has installed a keystroke logger into almost every senior manager's laptop. We walked into the system. Hell, they practically threw us a welcome party."

The meetings she arranged were her cover. Was he the only one around that meeting table who hadn't been compromised? No. Reuter refused to meet her. Did he know more than they thought?

"Without all that, though? Like at the prince's place?"

That twitch of the mouth again, that private joke betrayed for a moment. "Oh, we start with the weakest part of the network: email. The first step would be to find out the format for email and system usernames."

"How?"

"My preferred method is to contact customer services with a weird request. I'd ask if they can send me a copy of the allergen list for their menu or for their policy on employee social media use. In the prince's case, I asked for a letter to a local school who was doing a project on his home country. Anything that means a real person has to respond with an attached document."

"I don't understand."

"Documents have metadata, just like photographs. One of the pieces of information I can take from it is who created it. That tells me how your company formats their usernames. I need a real person to respond so I can see how they format their email usernames. Sometimes, it's different. If they're security conscious, they're different."

Asher started to understand. "So then you can hack their profile?"

"No. Then I can throw a bunch of passwords at it until something sticks. Ideally, we have lots of users and usernames that we chuck commonly used passwords at until one grants us access. With a bit of luck, you'll find that Bill from HR uses the same one for his emails as he does for everything else."

"Uh, is that a bad thing?"

Giulia groaned. "Oh, Asher. You better make more coffee, I'm going to be here a while."

Their mugs were empty, so Asher brought the cafetiere to the table and refilled them. "Keep telling me this stuff. It's interesting. What happens next?"

"Once I'm in Bill's email account, I'll send out a bunch of emails with my trojan horse attached. That's what gets me what I need to start making myself at home in the system."

"Can't you just do that from any account?"

"Some companies only allow internal email, or don't allow downloads from external sources. Even if they do, when you get an email from an unknown person, do you open the attachments?"

He shook his head, glad he could demonstrate even the most basic e-safety savvy. "No."

"Exactly. If someone from HR sends you an internal email with the title 'Holiday Entitlement Updates', would you open that?"

"Yeah," he admitted. He received emails like that all the time, he'd never thought twice before opening the attachment. Until now. "And you code all of these things? Sorry, my understanding of hackers comes from that scene in Swordfish with Hugh Jackman."

Giulia put her head on the table and pretended to sob.

"It's not like that in real life. For starters, code for things like this are open source. Hackers share their work so everyone else can use it. Which also means that the notion that hackers have some kind of unique identifier in their code is nonsense. Maybe in the past, when we had to code our own trojans, not now."

"Does Bonnie do this stuff, too?" Asher asked. There was an overwhelming amount to take in, he was worried he'd never catch up.

Giulia laughed. "No. She'd never admit it, but most of this goes over her head. She's not so good with the tech and theoretical side of it. Code confuses her. She's better with planning and doing the physical stuff, although, I believe you're aware of that." She winked almost imperceptibly, and his cheeks burned.

"She told you?"

"Bonnie doesn't let you into her confidence easily, but once you're there? She shares everything."

Something warm enveloped him at that. A feeling that he belonged to an elite group. It was a feeling he had to get used to.

By the time he was ready to leave for Bonnie's, Giulia had declared him 'something of a novice, but not a lost cause', which was more than he'd hoped for before she arrived. She walked out with him, refusing his offer of a lift.

When he got there, he double-checked the address, walking to the end of the street to reread the name, and zooming in and out of his maps app to clarify he was in the right place. The door didn't look like it concealed a house. When he knocked, he didn't expect an answer.

"Hi," she said. Her cheeks were flushed and she looked uncustomarily bashful. "Come in."

He did, feeling his own awkwardness in deciding if he should kiss her in greeting. "Uh, sorry I'm a little late. I thought I was lost, but I wasn't."

Move over Oscar Wilde, I am the next great orator.

She kissed him gently, with one hand on his cheek. His cheeks warmed.

"We're upstairs, in my office." Bonnie led the way past a chintzy but comfortable-looking sofa and chairs and an antique dresser filled with old china. "If you've spent the morning with Giuly, your brain will already be fried, I don't plan to do too much more damage."

At the top of the stairs, another staircase indicated further floors to the house. Asher mentally valued the property and almost choked at the figure. The landing opened out into a sort of workshop. It certainly wasn't an office like he'd been expecting. A long workbench took up the length of the wall, and one side held a vice, a selection of tools and a number of exenterated locks. On the other end, a drawing board displayed blueprints of a building he didn't recognise. Next to it, a pinboard was filled with notes. The radio played softly in the background, she must have been working here before he arrived.

For all that there was to take in, his attention was drawn to a small safe in the centre of the desk. This was to be the focus of the afternoon.

"Do I have to break into this?" He asked, already aware of the answer.

Bonnie patted the top of the safe. "Everyone has to start somewhere."

The fear he was experiencing must have been visible because her smile softened and she reached for a chunky padlock. "Sit," she said, doing likewise.

She handed him the lock. It was heavy, sturdy. The kind of thing he'd seen securing chains around gates on worksites. Asher looked back at Bonnie's expectant expression. "You want me to open this?"

"Security, for the most part, is an illusion. The locks we put on our doors, safes, cars and bikes are there to delay thieves, not stop them. An experienced locksmith could break in almost anywhere within minutes, and there are a lot of skilled criminals. You can develop the skills, too, Asher. All you have to do is change your perspective." Bonnie took the lock from him and tugged on it, demonstrating its strength. "Look for the weak points."

Asher's chin dropped as he watched her take two thin pieces of metal and jam them into either side of where the shackle connected with the body. It popped open.

"How did you do that?"

"I exploited the weakness." She turned back to the safe on the desk. "Now, I'll show you how to do the same with this."

It was easier than he thought. Much easier. He made a note to never used a hotel room safe again. Once he had the hang of breaking the safe, Bonnie showed him how to reset the combination. Then, she moved on to basic lifts and passes.

Distraction was the key, she told him. At the ball, she didn't take Reuter's phone when she was standing next to him, the lift happened when she bumped into him.

"I still think he'd have felt it," Asher said. "Given what we know about him, he must be aware of pickpockets."

Bonnie smirked. "Are you?"

"What do you mean? Of course, I'm aware."

"Check your pockets."

He did. Neither his phone or his wallet were where he left them. His wristwatch was missing, too. "How?"

"Distraction."

"More like confusion, you promised you wouldn't fry my brain."

"I lied. Sorry."

When she stood up, he spotted a little of the weariness he saw when they first met. No, the second time. He kept forgetting. The responsibilities on her were heavy, and he could see the burden she'd shouldered. He wanted to hold her and take the load away, even if just for a moment.

"Bonnie? We didn't get to finish our dance at the ball."

"I know."

He reached over and turned the radio's volume up. The sounds of a love song filled the room. "Do want to finish it now? I'd like to see how it ends."

She wound her arms around his shoulders and rested her head on his chest. He put his hands on her waist and let the music lead him. They swayed together, less elegantly than before, and he felt her move closer. He wrapped his arms around her, holding her tighter. Her heartbeat thumped against him and his matched hers. His brain felt cloudy; it was driving him on, encouraging him to be bold. When the song drew to an end, he stopped moving but didn't let her go. He wasn't sure he could.

Bonnie held her mouth close to his ear and spoke softly. "Asher? There's something you should know."

"What?" The possibilities flooded his mind, each one more upsetting than the last. He prepared himself for the worst.

"At Ahmed's, the alarm was triggered. I... I set it off to distract you. I wanted that diamond."

He should have been angry. A week ago, he would have been. Now, after everything he'd learned, all that he knew, instead of betrayal, he was relieved. He hadn't messed up by stealing the security pass, and he would have managed to successfully lift the diamond if Fitz hadn't sent a second, more skilled thief.

"Do you know what my final thought was, as you escaped that night? That the next time I met you, I'd be on top."

"As I remember it, I was on top that time, too."

He scooped her up into his arms as she laughed. "Well, it's definitely my turn now."

20

"Ready?" She looked at Asher, who was bouncing on the balls of his feet.

"As I'll ever be," he replied. "How about you?"

"I'm crapping myself, does that count?" Dhruv quipped.

"I was talking to Bon, but good to know, man."

Laughter burst through her earpiece, and her fists unclenched. The humour had broken the tension. Bonnie's heart slowed as the sweat pooling at the base of her spine ceased production. She'd never discussed the phenomenon of 'sweaty-heist-bum' with anyone else, and never would. Necessary secrets.

She checked her wrist. "Okay, the time on my watch is 22.59 and forty seconds. We move at 2300. Giuly? A countdown, please."

"10, 9, 8," Giulia's voice sounded solemn, focused.

Bonnie took a deep breath, blowing it out through pursed lips. She wiggled her fingers and tensed the muscles in her legs. This would be a marathon.

"7, 6, 5,"

She checked her pockets, feeling for the cloned keyfob, replica keys, autodialer, her picks and camera. They were all where they should be.

"4, 3, 2,"

Asher followed suit, patting his pockets for the hundredth time that evening.

"1. Let's do this." Giulia finished her countdown.

Bonnie approached the entrance and slid the straw of the duster spray through the gap at the top of the double doors. A quick squirt of the cooled gas fooled the sensors and the doors parted. Behind her, Asher whistled his appreciation.

"If that impressed you, prepare to have your mind blown tonight, Clueless," Giulia said through their earpieces. Bonnie allowed herself a smug smile.

This was it. Time to act. Bonnie nodded resolutely before walking through the doors. Asher followed her after a moment of hesitation. She removed the cloned pass from her pocket, scanned them both through the turnstiles and they walked smartly towards the elevator. He pushed the button, and the doors opened instantly.

"I guess everybody else is using the stairs at this time of day," he noted.

"God bless the working time directive," she said.

Inside the lift, Asher pushed the button for the floor two below their destination. Galvin's office was served by a separate elevator to which only he had a pass, so they had agreed to approach the rest of the way on foot. Only a select number of staff knew where he stored the pass card.

The doors opened, and they headed for the stairs. The access to the stairs, open during the day due to fire regulations, was locked. Bonnie reached for her pick set. She made short work of the lock with a wave rake. At least that one was easy.

"Bibi? You are good to go," Martin said.

Bonnie checked her watch. As planned, ten minutes had passed, they needed to get into Galvin's office as soon as possible. They ran up the stairs, finally grateful for Dhruv's relentlessness during training sessions, and arrived at Galvin's office.

Another locked door. She felt movement in the barrel as she tensioned it: security pins. This one was going to be trickier, so Bonnie abandoned the rake for a short hook. It took a few minutes, but the door soon opened. By now, her palms were clammy inside her gloves.

In the office, Asher retrieved the dictaphone from his pocket and held it close to the smart lock.

"Soteria." The voice that came out of the device was his father's. It was a testament to Giulia's software developing skills that Bonnie couldn't hear a trace of Asher in the phrasing. "Open the office door."

Two green lights flashed, the door clicked open.

"That freaks me out," She admitted.

"Giulia is disturbingly talented." He agreed, stuffing the dictaphone back in his jacket.

She handed him the metal cast of Galvin's key. Concerned about the strength of the 3D printed plastic version, Bonnie made a mould of it and cast another key. She had a file in her pick set to smooth out any inconsistencies; a mould of a print-out of a photographed key was never going to be a perfect match. Eyeing up the keyways, she pointed to the farthest lock. "Put the key in there and turn it slightly. How does it feel?"

Asher complied. "It's not moving."

"Show me." Asher handed her the key. She saw an indentation on the tip of one of the bits. An occupational hazard when you made copies from photographs. She filed it down until it was smooth again. "Try now."

Asher slid the key into the lock and shook his head. "Still nothing."

Once more, Bonnie filed down the offending bit. This time, Asher put it the lock and nodded; the key moved slightly from its initial position. Without the other key, it would never go all the way, but the movement showed her that it would turn when ready.

"Hold your breath," she said as Asher handed her a blue spray bottle. She lightly sprayed a solution of ninhydrin and acetone over the safe's keypad. It was a fine mist, but it would take time to dry. Time that she could use to work on the second lock. Asher stood guard, shining the torch on the keypad, watching for a reaction.

Crouching in front of the second-to-last lock of the day, she analysed it. Like its partner, it had an evil paracentric keyway; deep zigzags that most standard picks would be too large to pass. She reached for the picks she had customised for the occasion from a pair of old windscreen wiper blades — a long, deep hook and a shallow tension wrench. Tensioning the lock, she reached to the back of the keyway and worked her way forward, feeling for binding pins. Her finely filed pick slid between the wards and she felt the first pin set into place. Eight more to go. Another minute passed, she managed to set a further 4 pins. She was past the halfway mark and picking up speed. Each pin took its place, Bonnie felt the movement in the tips of her fingers, the tension rod affirming what the hook told her.

At the final pin, she spoke. "Asher, turn the key on my word." He grabbed the brass key, still in the lock where he'd left it, waiting on her command. The binding pin clicked into place, and the tension rod jumped against her finger, "Go"

Bonnie let out a long slow breath as both wrench and key turned in unison. *One (two?) down.* She shone her light on the keypad, five keys were now smudged with purple dye.

"We have five digits, Martin," Asher said. Bonnie connected the autodialer to the keypad and input the numbers 1, 2, 5, 9, 0.

"You need six. All Alconbury keypads have six-digit codes. Is one of the numbers more smudged or more deeply stained than the others?" Martin suggested.

After examining the numbers again, Bonnie hit 9 a second time and pushed send. The autodialer burst into life. Countless combinations of the numbers played across the screen so quickly it looked like a blur. After only a few moments, a shrill beep told them that the device had done its job. Martin was a genius. Bonnie knew this type of safe cracking was beyond her capabilities.

Safe open, Asher and Bonnie systematically checked the contents. The pocket watch was inside a suitably luxurious velvet case. Asher opened it and they 'ooh'ed at its beauty.

"It's your turn to go, be safe." She turned to Asher. It looked like he was going to object, and she readied herself for an argument. After a pause, he nodded and jogged towards the door. "Dhruv? Asher is on his way. Prepare the rooftop escape."

"On it," Dhruv said.

Alone in the office, Bonnie ensured she had everything she needed. She knew there wouldn't be another chance to access the safe so easily. After tonight, the security at Anderson HQ would be significantly beefier. Satisfied, she disconnected the autodialer and stowed it back in her jacket. She removed her picks from the locks and let the door swing shut; the keypad trilled, letting her know that it had reengaged.

"Asher is out," Dhruv informed her.

Bonnie's relief that Asher was safe was fleeting, she still had her own escape to negotiate. "Good. Get yourself clear, too, Dhruv. Bibi, get ready to go."

"On your signal," Bianca said.

"Bonnie? Are you ready?" Giulia asked.

"Hit the kill switch. Everyone? Get the hell out of here." Bonnie braced herself for what came next.

"Done and done."

Then, alarm bells started blaring.

Within minutes, flashing lights outside flooded into the building.

Bonnie was trapped.

~ ~ ~

Asher was at the corner of the street when the alarm sounded. Martin and Giulia pulled up across the road. He dashed over to get into the car.

"Are the others safe?" He asked.

The pause before either of them spoke told him more than their words did.

"Bianca is taking the back roads to the Warren Street Station, and Dhruv went the opposite way to Goodge Street. He's already on the train," Giulia said. When she turned back to him, her smile was forced, her teeth clenched.

A police car sped past them in the opposite direction.

"And Bonnie?" Asher prompted.

"Her earpiece went quiet the minute the alarm went off."

Cold fear gripped his windpipe. He wanted to lean forward and grab the steering wheel, wanted to turn the car around and go back for her.

Anticipating this, Martin reminded him. "We follow the plan."

"I know," Asher said.

They would rendezvous at Bonnie's house, as agreed. Fitz was already there, Giulia would drop him and Martin off before parking the car in Chinatown. Bianca and Dhruv would arrive when they could.

Bonnie... Would she be there?

It didn't take long to get there, Seven Dials was relatively close to Fitzrovia, and at this late hour, the roads were empty. Which meant the police would be on the scene within minutes of the alarm triggering.

Martin opened the door with his own set of keys, waving to Giulia to let her know they were in. She flashed her lights as she passed them. Inside, he heard deep voices carry up the stairs. Martin kicked off his trainers where several other pairs lay. Asher removed his shoes and added them to the collection.

"This way," Martin pointed to the staircase.

As Asher followed, the voices grew louder; he could hear a jovial edge to the conversation. How were they so relaxed? At the base of the stairs, the room opened out into a bright kitchen he hadn't seen yet. A large, green-blue range cooker dominated the space behind a long wooden dining table. The chairs and benches that surrounded it were cushioned in mismatched patterns, although the fabric looked expensive. It was homely.

Around the table, Fitz, Lucy and Dhruv sat, each clutching a mug. Dhruv jumped up and immediately kissed and hugged Martin, relief showing on both of their faces.

Fitz held up his phone. "Bianca is on her way. She's leaving the Tube station now."

Asher nodded numbly. Nobody was asking about Bonnie. She was still inside the building when the alarm went off and no one, but Asher seemed to care. How was she going to get out?

Noticing his concern, Lucy stood. "I'm going to make more tea. Asher, will you help me?"

"Uh, sure," he said, grateful for something to do.

Lucy filled the kettle with water and set it on the hob. It was one of the old fashioned types with a whistle on the spout, it would take time to boil.

"Are you okay?" Lucy asked, leaning against the counter.

"No," he admitted. "She was still inside the building and we left her there. Why aren't we doing something?"

A smile flashed briefly over her lips. "What do you want to do? Storm the building? Ride in on a white horse, bedecked in armour?"

"To clarify, who is wearing the armour, me or the horse?"

"Does that change the answer?"

The corners of his mouth lifted and his mood grew lighter. "Yes. If the horse is wearing it, then yeah, I want to see that."

"It'll take some time to source the horse, but honestly, if anyone can get us a ceremonial horse in full battle regalia, it's Jim," Lucy said. Asher laughed. "Seriously though, we have to trust that Bonnie has a plan. I know it's hard, I've been in your place many times. I'm always going to worry about her, but I've done this often enough to know that she knows what she's doing."

~ ~ ~

Giulia's research had been correct. The time from the alarm triggering and the police response was almost exactly as she predicted it. Four minutes and forty-five seconds, by Bonnie's watch. She had made it to the first-floor cleaning cupboard as the siren started blaring. She was past the lock and had changed her clothes as the first set of flashing lights shone through the window and down the polished marble hallway.

Impersonating a police officer was a criminal offence. Doing so at a crime scene was probably considered worse. For the extra six months on her sentence, if caught, it was worth the risk to get away. The police were expecting a rooftop escape. Dhruv gave them that. If all went to plan, they'd be surrounding the exits of the building across the street while a masked blonde ran in the opposite direction. CCTV would confirm that the Met's finest had been looking in the wrong direction.

Bonnie would have to wait until they started their sweep of this building before she could leave. It could be a while longer. In the meantime, she had some evidence bags to prepare.

It felt like an age, but in reality, it was no more than an hour until HQ was a hive of activity. A trail of uniformed officers began to work their way up the corridor, trying doors and checking inside rooms. The door in front of her rattled, and Bonnie was glad that her little closet locked from the inside. She waited until the last step of echoing footsteps had faded away before slipping out of her hiding place.

The tall Asian one with a slim face and neat beard. That was all she had to go on as she scanned the officers littering the lobby. She found him, talking to Galvin, serious expressions on their faces. Bonnie moved to avoid their line of sight, watching them. He looked young to be out of uniform; there was a wide-eyed quality to his gaze that made Bonnie sure he was mentally pinching himself every so often for being in his position. It was doubtlessly exacerbated by Galvin's stature and entitlement.

When DI Stewart, the one in charge of the taskforce, relieved him, Bonnie watched as he retreated to the opposite end of the lobby, as far as possible from Galvin. She followed him.

"DC Maamoud? I was told to give this to you." Bonnie held out the evidence bag, complete with fake details filled out on the side.

Maamoud took it between his index and middle finger like it might be contaminated. "Thanks. I'll get this to the boss."

Bonnie didn't wait to make sure he did.

It was time to go.

~ ~ ~

"I'm baaaaack."

Asher's heart leapt in his chest before sinking into the pit of his stomach again when the light footsteps on the stairs revealed themselves to belong to Bianca, not Bonnie.

Bianca, it turned out, did know the whole story. She and Bonnie shared more than a predilection for breaking locks and a privileged upbringing. It turned out that Fitz and Bonnie had helped Bianca and her father out of a tricky situation involving a tabloid journalist and a crooked police officer, some years ago. Bianca had been hoping for a chance to repay the favour.

As Bonnie had explained: "the taskforce have a pencil sketch of a basis of a working theory. We need to confirm a few hunches for them. One, in particular, is the identity of the blonde woman in the hat and mask at the last scene."

After a detour to Human Resources for one specific file, Bianca made sure to leave through the fire exit. It was wired to the security systems, and opening it would trigger an alarm. It was also covered by closed-circuit television, the footage maintained by a private contractor. She made sure to stick to surveilled streets until the first police cars began to show up. Then, she headed for a dimly lit alleyway to shed her mask and leather jacket before catching public transport back to Bonnie's house.

"The gang's all here," Dhruv said.

Asher's stomach flipped. They were all speaking as if Bonnie wasn't coming back. Fitz and Giulia were talking about making supper for everyone and discussing who should sleep in which bedroom. He was about to say something, call out this odd nihilist behaviour, when his phone trilled.

"Asher, there's been an incident at the office. I need to you get here as soon as." Galvin ended the call before Asher could respond. When he looked up, the entire room was looking at him.

"Was that Bonnie?" Martin asked. His face, like all the rest, revealed concern.

They were all worried about her.

"Uh, no. It was my father. I've been summoned to the office."

"Did we plan for this?" Fitz asked.

"A through Z, Jim," Lucy said, covering for Bonnie. There was no plan for this. "Asher knows what to do and how to act."

"What's concerning is that neither he nor Bon thought Galvin would call. They both believed he'd ring Reuter before Asher," Dhruv explained.

"Ah, I see. That is interesting." Fitz scratched his chin. "I wonder what changed?"

"About that..."

In the aftermath of Galvin's phone call, nobody was listening out for the door. Bonnie had crept down the stairs unnoticed. He startled at the police uniform in his peripheral vision before remembering the plan.

Her eyes locked with his, relief evident on her face. He ran to her and was kissing her before he considered their audience. Wolf-whistles and cheers surrounded them, but he couldn't bring himself to be embarrassed. She was safe, that was all that mattered.

"Did you get the watch?" Martin asked.

"No," Bonnie said.

"What? After all that, we didn't even get what we came for?"

"Oh, we got exactly what we needed. Speaking of which, you should go to your father, Asher."

Asher frowned, not sure what she meant by that. Whatever it was, he would find out soon enough.

21

The air was crisp, and the blue flashing lights hung eerily in the late-night mist. Springtime might be warming up the days, but the nights were still cold. Fliss wished she'd considered that as she'd thrown on some clothes while Maamoud waited outside her building. She pulled the collar of her jacket closer together and shivered.

Fliss hadn't seen this many police officers in one place since the last department Christmas party. Arif gave up on trying to push his Prius through the assembled squad cars and abandoned the vehicle to walk towards the main entrance. Galvin Anderson, the CEO of the company whose headquarters this was, was already there, speaking officiously to a terrified-looking uniformed sergeant. Fliss took pity on him and interrupted, introducing herself.

"Mr Anderson, I'm Detective Inspector Stewart, I'm the officer in charge here.

His eyes widened at her introduction. There was a beat, he restored his previous expression of mild annoyance. "Can you tell me what's happening, then?"

"Forgive me, I've just arrived, so I need to catch up on the details. From what I've been told, however, there has been a robbery in the building. At least, an attempted robbery. Once I speak to the responding officer, I'll be able to give you more."

Anderson huffed, blue lights in the air made him look as cold as Fliss felt. His grey eyes were like ice. "Fine."

"Constable Maamoud? Could you stay with Mr Anderson just now, please? Then, we'll make a list of anyone who would have access to the offices at this time of day. Perhaps you could try to contact the head of security."

Arif nodded and pulled his notebook from his pocket. Fliss heard his opening question to Anderson as she strode down the lobby towards DI Ingram, the CID detective who was initially called to the scene. He contacted Fliss when he noticed the zipline between the offices and the building opposite. It matched her burglar's MO.

"Hey, thanks for calling me in on this. Do we know what's missing?" She asked.

Ingram frowned. "Don't thank me yet. We haven't found anything amiss. I've got guys on every exit of the bank across the road, but nobody has tried to leave. Uniforms are moving up through the floors here, trying to clear the building. So far, so normal."

"False alarm?" Fliss thought out loud.

"I wish. The alarm system has certain failsafes to stop accidental call outs. It wouldn't have dialled the police without good reason. Now, it might still turn out to be very big mice, but I doubt it."

On cue, Ingram's radio sounded. "Sir, I think we found something. We're in an office on the third floor."

"I'm on my way," he confirmed. "Are you coming, Stewart?"

Fliss nodded. "I'll meet you there. I should placate the CEO first. He might be able to shed some light on whatever your guys have found if he's feeling amenable."

"Good call."

She smiled. Ingram was one of the good ones. He called her in specifically so she knew he wouldn't try to steal credit if Fliss's crook was behind this. As it stood, she didn't think it would go that far. Her suspect (for all that she had had one) had never targeted an office building before. What could possibly be in here to steal? There was one person who knew the answer.

"Mr Anderson, thank you for waiting." She excused Arif and turned to meet Galvin's insistent stare. "We believe that a break-in did occur this evening, and that the thieves made a rooftop escape. What I need to know from you is what you believe somebody would be here to steal."

Anderson baulked. It was a reaction Fliss was used to. Even if you were expecting the question, something was jarring about listing all the reasons why you might be a victim of a crime. In this case, however, it went deeper than that. Anderson was reticent to share those reasons with her in particular.

"There is nothing in here of resale value, if that's what you're suggesting. There are many valuable assets, however, in the way of people, ideas, information. If this is some kind of corporate sabotage, I'm not sure that I'm happy to tell you exactly what they might wish to take."

"I understand, Mr Anderson. Is there any person or company that comes to mind in regards to sabotage?"

"Not off the top of my head."

A familiar prickling sensation reignited a memory. A similarly reticent attitude from Prince Amhed when she questioned him about his missing diamond. If Rez hadn't explained why Ahmed was acting coy, she might still be in the dark about it. Maybe he had some insight into this situation, too?

Before she could ask Galvin anything further, her radio hissed into life. "DI Stewart, I think you should see what we found up here."

"Thanks, I'm on my way." Fliss looked at Galvin. "My officers have found something that I need to look at. Let me find someone to stay with you while I deal with this."

"Can I call someone? My head of security? My lawyer? My Chief Commercial Officer? Somebody else from my team? I don't like being questioned alone." Anderson was already pulling out his phone.

There was no reason he shouldn't, but Fliss wanted to delay him. The inkling that he was hiding something made her want to keep him isolated from allies for a little longer. "Actually, why don't you come up with me. You might be able to help us to make sense of what we found."

"Fine." Galvin huffed and rolled his eyes. He wasn't used to being told what to do.

Fliss led him towards the lifts, noticing Maamoud lurking behind a pillar, waiting to talk to her. He looked like a toddler who needed the bathroom. She and Galvin were stepping in through the sliding doors when Arif made his move and stopped her.

"Ma'am, I've been handed something that you should see." His eyes flitted between her and Galvin, not wanting to include him in this. Anderson was too close now, Fliss had chosen to involve him.

Fliss took the evidence bag from him and had to double-take. It made no sense. "What is this?"

Arif shrugged. "One of the officers found it in the hallway. I don't know what to make of it."

"Fuck."

In a single whispered word, Anderson said more than he had all evening. He knew what this pencil sketch was. It looked like a scribbled diagram of a pocket watch: an expert scribble, but nothing more detailed than that.

"Mr Anderson, do you know what this could be?" Fliss held the evidence bag out to him, pretending she hadn't already heard his reaction. He shook his head, ashen-faced.

As the lift doors closed, Fliss saw Arif raise his eyebrows and flip open his notebook. When the lift reached the third floor, she started to step out of the elevator, but Anderson hung back.

"I, uh, need to check on something in my office." He pushed another button. Fliss blocked the doors with her foot.

"Mr Anderson, the other floors haven't been cleared yet, the perpetrators might still be in the building. I can't let you go up without accompanying you."

He paused. Fliss watched him weigh up his options. Something important was in his office, something he needed to check on now that he'd seen the sketch of the watch. Whatever it was, Fliss wanted to see it, too.

Anderson sighed. "Fine."

The lift took them to the top, but when they exited, Fliss saw that there was a flight of stairs, leading them further up. She followed Anderson's hasty steps until they reached a door. He audibly inhaled before depressing the handle. It gave way, and the door swung open. Anderson whimpered.

"What's wrong?" She asked.

"That should be locked." His voice cracked. He stepped forward to another door and spoke into a discrete grey speaker. "Soteria, open the office door."

When the door popped open, Anderson rushed through, ignoring Fliss. He yelped at whatever was on the other side. She found him, gawping at the hefty safe in the corner of the room. The keypad had purplish smudges on specific keys which she recognised immediately as ninhydrin. The crime scene techs used it to reveal fingerprints; the chemical reacted to amino acids. Until he pointed lower, she hadn't noticed what was bothering him. One lock had a rough-looking brass key sticking out of it.

"Is that usually in there?"

Anderson shook his head. "No. That's where my key goes." He pulled a bunch of keys from his pocket and separated out a zagged silver one. "But this is my key."

"Who has the other?"

"My Chief Commercial Officer. My friend, Kieran."

That, too, was interesting. She grabbed her radio. "Ingram?" It hissed. "I've been detained and can't get to the third floor. What did you find?"

"It's the Human Resources records room. The window was smashed to enter the room and one file drawer was bent until the lock snapped. Only one file was removed, though. Its contents were jammed in the shredder."

"What file?"

A double beep initiated the Pavlovian response of reaching for her phone. The message was from Arif. That was strange, he would usually call, or use the radio. When she opened the text, she realised why he opted for this method. He had managed to get a list of the people whose security pass had accessed the building after office hours. One name was somebody she'd encountered before.

Ingram's voice sounded through the radio. "The file belongs to one Reuter, Kieran."

That confirmed her hunch.

"Okay, let's go bring Kieran Reuter in for questioning."

22

"Do you really think he was trying to steal from you?" Asher asked again. He couldn't believe that Galvin had turned on his friend so quickly.

"If you have a better explanation, I'd love to hear it, Asher," Galvin said. With every response, he became less patient. "Can we get on with this?"

Galvin went back to reading the report Asher made for him. It was as inconsequential as every other report he'd made, but his father was suddenly interested in his input. Reuter had been questioned by the police at home. They hadn't detained him, there wasn't enough evidence to do anything further. In the eyes of the law, Kieran was innocent; as far as Galvin was concerned, he was guilty as hell.

All day, Asher saw Reuter lurking in corridors, waiting for a chance to speak to Galvin. Presumably, he wanted to explain the situation. The man had been set up, after all; he truly was innocent. Regardless, Galvin had spent the day actively ignoring Kieran.

We Bear A Grudge.

Kieran was no longer in Galvin's inner circle. Asher had, apparently, taken his place. They were uncomfortable shoes to fill.

Galvin hadn't exactly come clean to Asher about the attempted robbery. He didn't mention the watch. He merely told Asher that somebody had copied his key and had tried to access the safe. The forensics team found scratches inside the lock that suggested that the moulded copy wasn't a good fit for the lock. Nobody could say for sure if the safe was opened and Galvin was pinning all his hopes on that.

The watch box was currently nestled inside Galvin's briefcase, ready to be transported to the penthouse after work. It was already five o'clock on Friday, Galvin would be leaving soon.

Asher checked his phone. What was holding up Bonnie?

~ ~ ~

"The police were at my house again."

He slammed his office door and loomed over her, blocking her way out. Anger contorted his face and Bonnie's muscles tensed, ready to fight back if necessary.

"Again?" Bonnie played dumb, she wasn't meant to know about the first visit. "Why?"

"None of your business."

"So why am I here?"

"I know what you did," Kieran said. Spittle gathered in white globs at the corners of his mouth, making Bonnie's stomach turn.

"I don't know what you mean."

He moved closer, now inches from her face. "My phone. Your friend fucked with it at the ball. Then my card was used to get into the building for an attempted robbery. I know you're involved."

She had to give him kudos for joining the dots.

"What do you think happened to your phone? And how. The. Fuck. Does that have anything to do with your card?"

In a moment of hesitation, he stepped back, giving Bonnie space to breath again. She relaxed her defensive stance slightly.

"All I know is that I did not leave it in my jacket pocket, but when I found it there, it was switched off. My phone is always on."

"And that means my friend tampered with it?" She scoffed. "That's quite a stretch."

"It was in my pocket!"

Bonnie kept her tone even, her words slow. She needed to diffuse the situation somehow. "Do you have any idea how many people were at that ball? I mean, was my date ever even near you? Close enough to take something from your pocket without you noticing? You're a switched on guy, I can't believe anyone could do that to you."

Men like Kieran thought they were the smartest person in every room, especially compared to someone younger, female or not white. "It's just..."

"Tell me, is your assumption based on his vicinity to me, or is it more sinister? I mean, of all the people there, you instantly assume the black guy did it?"

Kieran baulked. "How dare you!"

"Let me guess, your good friend is black, right?"

"No, I. No!" It was a low blow, but now, he was on the defensive.

"Give me some evidence. Otherwise, I'll be forced to think you're profiling him for the wrong reasons." She shrugged and leaned back in her chair. He sputtered in indignation. "This card you mentioned? Did my friend steal that, too? Was it also in your jacket? And, if so, how have you been getting into the office every day since?"

Kieran glared at her, jaw twitching as he ground his teeth. He had nothing concrete, Bonnie could tell. If he did, he would have been armed with evidence instead of throwing vague allegations around. *She* was the one who stole his phone. *She* broke into his hotel room and cloned his access card. Martin did tamper with the phone, that much was true, but on the scale of things, he was least guilty.

"You think you're smart? That you've 'got me'? You have no idea what you're digging into, missy."

In her pocket, she pressed record on her dictaphone. "Enlighten me, what am I digging into?"

Goaded, he was primed to start peacocking. "I run things around here. You think Galvin is in charge because his name is on the place? I'm the one who raised the cash to start the first hotel. I'm the one pulling all the strings. I have dirt on every single person in this organisation, especially Galvin. I own him. Whatever you think you have on me, I have ten times as much on you. I will expose you."

She shouldn't have done it, but he annoyed her. Bonnie laughed. A contemptuous cackle that portrayed her scorn for him. He was a bully, and she had little time for men like him.

"You have nothing on me," she said after the laughter subsided. "If you did, I wouldn't be in your office. You'd have taken this to Galvin or the police."

"You don't get to laugh at me, bitch," he spat. "If you won't confess to me, you can explain yourself to Galvin."

He stormed from the room, leaving her behind. A click told her he'd locked the door behind himself, trapping her in the office.

Insulted that he thought a locked door would stop her from leaving, she considered the ramifications of that. He didn't know anything about her. If he did, he would have known her proficiency with locks.

It looked like she was going to be there a while, so she got to work.

The computer screen was still lit, the system not yet in standby. She wiggled the mouse to make sure it didn't go to sleep. No password requests popped up. If anyone in the company had a secure password, it would be Kieran. She wasn't sure Giulia's password attacks would give her any results in the timeframe she had. Bonnie retrieved a blank USB from her bag and got ready to plug it into the processor. She would take everything and sift through it later.

It was, however, likely that Reuter would store confidential files in an obscure part of this desktop, not on the cloud where anyone could accidentally open it. Unless he had encrypted the data, of course. Then Giulia and Martin would be pulling an all-nighter to break the encryption.

That thought prompted her to dig out a different flash drive — one of Giulia's. This one imitated a human interface drive, like a keyboard or a mouse to deliver a key-logger to the system. Giulia had coded it to email the information to an untraceable email account every hour; it also grabbed files and folders from the desktop and sent them to a remote server. If nothing else, they might discover his passwords and let Giulia in to dig around in the network. Out of interest, she browsed his recently opened documents. If he was storing information in a random rich text file, it should still show up there.

Bonnie glanced at the clock. Kieran had been gone five minutes already. If her calculations were correct and the elevators were running smoothly, he should be reaching Galvin's office door soon. Could she stall him? Perhaps.

She dialled Galvin's direct line, he picked up after two rings. "Hello"

"Mr Anderson! I'm glad I caught you. You're not too busy, are you?"

"I'm just wrapping up a meeting with Asher—"

She cut across him "That's handy because I'm meeting with him soon and was calling to get some clarification on what you want his social media strategy to look like."

"Oh, well, I have discussed it with him a little, so he'll be able to explain it when you meet. From my point of view, I want him to be more statesmanlike. I want people to take him seriously."

"Excellent." She pretended to take notes. "Actually, if Asher is there, can I speak to him for a moment, please?"

After background muttering and scuffling as the phone handset was passed over. "Hi?"

"Hey, Asher, funny story. I'm locked in Reuter's office, and he's on his way to summon your father and tell him that *I* broke into his office."

"What? Why?"

"My guess? He misses being the favourite. And Galvin knows where they keep the ducking stool. Stall him, please?"

His tone changed to breezy. She could hear him trying to pretend there was no problem. "Okay, then meet me in my office. As soon as you can?"

"Will do. Just give me as much time as possible."

She hung up before Galvin could speak to her again. Two dialogue boxes were waiting for her on the screen, telling her that the file transfer and keyloggers were finished doing their jobs. She put both back in her bag and forced the system to sleep. From this side of the door, she was able to easily shim the latch open with a plastic card she kept in her purse for such occasions.

There was a queue at the lifts so Bonnie took the stairs, bounding up two storeys as quickly and quietly as possible. Asher's office was at the end of the corridor, just before the open-plan customer service area. Under the cover of ambient office noise and several phone conversations, she turned the door handle.

It was locked.

Chuckling to herself, she reached for her pick set, one more time.

~ ~ ~

Asher tried to keep his face neutral as he hung up the phone and settled back into his seat opposite Galvin.

"All okay?" Galvin asked.

"Yeah," he said, voice too high. "Bonnie just wanted to move up our meeting."

Outside the office, he heard voices. Kieran was talking to Andrew, demanding to see Galvin. With relief, he heard Andrew deny him access. "Mr Anderson is in a meeting right now. If you want to wait a few minutes, he shouldn't be much longer."

Asher's heart thumped in his chest. There was nothing left to discuss with his father, but he needed to stall Kieran. Actually, there was one thing left to discuss. It was something he wanted to avoid. *I hope you appreciate this, Bonnie.* He braced himself.

"Uh, dad? Uncle Rami called me this morning. He said he heard about the robbery, but you're not returning his calls. What's up?"

Galvin's jaw tensed. He spoke from between clenched teeth. "I have nothing to discuss with Ramirez."

"How do you know if you won't listen to what he has to say?"

"Asher," Galvin snapped. "I do not have to justify my reasons to anyone, least of all, you."

"Wow, dad. That's a sentiment every son wants to hear."

Asher stood up and started towards the door. His father sighed audibly. Asher paused, his hand on the door handle. Galvin never let him have the last word, so he waited.

"Tell him I'll answer the call next time, okay?"

Asher smiled at the door and nodded. "Thanks."

He slipped out of the office, closing the door behind him. In Andrew's little workspace, Kieran was pacing in front of the desk. Asher imagined it would be an intimidating situation for the assistant and decided to have some fun.

"Kieran! Everything sorted with the police? I have to say, it was a shock to all of us that you were involved with the robbery."

A low growl sounded in Kieran's throat as he glanced nervously at Andrew. Galvin hadn't mentioned Kieran's link to the robbery to anyone except Asher. Andrew was an unstoppable gossip. By the end of the day, the entire support staff would know he'd been implicated. It wouldn't matter that he was innocent (of this particular crime, at least), he'd be everybody's number one suspect.

He didn't respond to Asher. Kieran pushed his way past and barged into Galvin's office before Andrew could alert his boss to the visitor. The assistant blanched, expecting fallout. The voices in the office sounded heated, but nobody emerged. Asher should go. He needed a head start.

"Andrew? Could you do something for me?" The young man nodded. "When Galvin comes out of the office, can you find something urgent for him to deal with or look at?"

"I have some leave requests for him to sign, would that do?"

"Perfect. You're a genius," Asher shouted from the hall as he sprinted towards the stairwell. He took the stairs two at a time in his haste to reach his office before Kieran convinced Galvin to do whatever he had planned for Bonnie. He shivered. Her ducking stool quip was probably not far from the truth.

As he reached his office, he pulled the key from his pocket before reconsidering. He told Bonnie to meet him there, the door wouldn't be locked any more. It swung open, Bonnie was sitting on his desk, legs swinging.

"About time!" She joked.

Relief or concern or some other unrealised emotion made him do it. He wasn't in control. He raced towards the desk and kissed her. She kissed him back, grabbing his jacket and pulling him closer.

"We shouldn't be doing this, it's against all the rules," she murmured, as his teeth grazed her neck. He pulled her blouse from her pencil skirt and pushed his hands underneath. Electricity sparked in his fingers where they touched her. "We should stop. It's not a good idea."

It might be close to the end of the day on Friday, but while Galvin was in his office, everyone was still at their desks. Add to that, Kieran was on the warpath, searching the building for Bonnie. He would come looking for her on this floor, eventually.

"Mmhmm." Finding the zip of her skirt, he unfastened it and slid the black jersey fabric down her legs. She kicked it across the room. When he glanced down, his heart jumped to see she was wearing stockings. He groaned. "We have time."

Asher crouched by her legs, running his hands up the smooth fabric, kissing the exposed skin on her thighs where the nylon ended. He put his pinkie under the strap of her suspender belt and followed the satin line upwards until he reached the lace that encircled her waist, pushing her blouse up, out of his way. His tongue traced the outline of her abs, and she tensed her stomach, gasping and raking her fingers through his hair.

"Really, Asher, we're not meant to be here. We definitely shouldn't be doing this." She said.

"You're right." Asher's voice was breathless. "But I don't want to stop, do you?"

He stood to face her, pulling her into a deep kiss. She grazed his bottom lip with her teeth as her urgency grew, and his brain handed the reins to someplace further south.

She unbuttoned his shirt and ran her fingertips across his abdomen, towards his waistband. His muscles fluttered whenever her expert fingers hit his sweet spots. He removed her blouse and dropped it where his shirt had landed. His trousers followed, and Asher stepped out of his shoes to kick them off in the same direction as their shirts.

Asher lay Bonnie across the desk, clearing the surface by sweeping the items noisily to the floor in one swift movement. He climbed above her, kissing up her sternum, tugging on her bra with his teeth before continuing and lingering at the crook of her neck to nip and suck at one particularly sensitive place. He knew it would leave a mark. He didn't care, he loved hearing the gasps and moans she made in response to his mouth.

She drew her nails up his spine, the delicious sensation making him arch his back, grinding his hips into her.

"Asher!" A shocked voice sounded from the, apparently still unlocked, office door. "Miss Duncan?"

"Father." Asher turned to face the man.

"Mr Anderson?" Bonnie was less brazen.

"Get dressed, right now," Galvin said furiously. "Then go home. Separately. I will deal with this tomorrow."

"But, father, tomorrow is Saturday. Shouldn't this wait until Monday?" Asher's tone was full of bravado he didn't feel.

"No, you will come to the penthouse at nine o'clock tomorrow. Both of you. Now, Asher, my driver will take you home. Miss Duncan, I trust you can find your own way back?"

Galvin's tone dripped of 'I'm not angry, I'm disappointed', while his eyes read pure embarrassment. That he'd walked in on this, witnessed by Reuter, was worse than if he'd stumbled on them alone.

Bonnie managed to sound contrite. "Yes, sir, I'm... sorry."

Kieran looked jubilant at this misstep. He surely believed that his own misdemeanours would be diminished by comparison. Asher almost felt sorry for him.

Almost.

23

Bonnie winked at Asher and he smiled nervously. The elevator attendant wasn't watching, but the mirrored surfaces of the lift meant he could see them even with his back turned. In the reflection, she saw him grin. As far as he knew, they were an enamoured couple. In reality, they were two employees riding towards their fate.

The awkwardness of being caught in her underwear by her boss had been outweighed by the thrill of what went before. The situation might have been contrived, but the passion was real. Her stomach flipped whenever she recalled it.

Galvin had been furious in that dangerously calm way. Simmering under the surface, ready to explode when the moment allowed. He couldn't scream at them in the office, not with the entire customer service team within earshot. Not in front of Kieran. In that moment, he couldn't deal with them the way he wanted to. Today, in his own home, he could dole out his punishment. Bonnie hoped that he'd calmed down overnight. Perhaps time would dampen his anger. At the very least, she hoped he'd go easy on Asher.

"Where's Candy and Co?" Asher asked.

"She's shopping. I didn't think she should have to hear about this."

"Ah, yes. We must shield her from adult life, mustn't we?"

Bonnie hid her snort behind a cough. Huffy indignance was a family trait.

"You seem to require time to calm down, Asher. I will speak to Miss Duncan first." Galvin held the door for her. "After you."

"Of course," she said.

Asher caught her eye, panicking. They'd both expected him to call Asher first. Plans 'A through Z' wouldn't be necessary, however; this was merely a variation on plan A. As she passed, she held the tool kit behind her back for Asher. The last thing she saw before Galvin closed the door was his pale, terrified face. She hoped he was up to the job.

"Miss Duncan," Galvin said, sitting on the only armchair in the room. Bonnie stood. "You came highly recommended. Other employers told me how effective, how motivating and how professional you were. I can only hope this was a blip in that promised professionalism."

Bonnie nodded. This was a rehearsed speech, it was only fair to let him finish it. "Yes, sir."

"I have rules for a reason, and I expect every employee to follow them, no matter how exceptional their references. My son is included in that, and I will deal with him, too. However, as far as I'm concerned in this matter, Miss Duncan, you are no longer an employee of Anderson Hotels."

It was to be expected. Bonnie knew the consequences. The job had been a ruse, a way to access information, but she didn't particularly want a stain on her resume. "I understand, Mr Anderson. I'm sorry it ended like this."

"As am I."

"I know it's not my place, but you're not going to fire Asher, are you? This was my fault. I'd hate to see his career come to an end because of one, small indiscretion."

"Well, I'd hate to see that, too. If you're willing to take full responsibility for this debacle, then perhaps I can overlook Asher's part in it."

She forced a smile. "Of course. And, for your part, I would hope that this incident wouldn't be discussed should any future employer contact you for a reference?"

"I'm sure I can arrange that. Now, you may send Asher in here on your way out."

"Thank you, Mr Anderson."

She pulled the door to as she left, concealing the pass between her and Asher. The box was bigger than she remembered, it only just fit in her bag.

At the exit, Asher called back to her. "I'll see you around."

'Around', was at Uncle Jim's. Asher met her there shortly after she arrived. Instead of taking them into the office, Jim invited them into his cosy sitting room.

"There are too many of us to fit comfortably in the study."

They'd managed fine in the past with three in that room, so Bonnie was already preparing herself for a surprise as they entered and found someone was already waiting for them.

"Rami?!" Asher exclaimed.

The man nodded. Behind the suave and confident exterior, he wore concern. Bonnie took pity on him and extended her hand.

"Hi, Rez, it's good to see you again."

Asher gawped as Rez shook her hand and smiled. "And you, Bonnie. I take it you've worked this all out?"

"You're Asher's uncle, right? The jeweller." Rez nodded as Asher jerked his head, still catching up with the new information. "You made the forgery?"

"In my defence, I didn't know it was going to be switched for the real Coronation Watch. I was young and stupid when I stole it. I just wanted the challenge, then I was going to return it to the museum. When I discovered the truth from my sister, I tried to make amends."

"But... Reuter." Asher stammered.

"Is everything you suspected him to be and more. He was trying to extort Prince Ahmed for his diamond. There was a bidding war and he decided to cut out the middle man. When that didn't work, he thought blackmail would." Fitz sat back in his chair.

Bonnie and Rez sat, too. Asher continued to stand. "What about dad?"

"He's been covering for Reuter for decades. False alibis, arranging 'business trips' when he needed to travel to suspicious countries, fronting him the cash when he needs large sums. Reuter gives him a cut. Alicia told me about it, she overheard more than enough to take them both down."

"And then she had her breakdown."

A solemn nod. "She wasn't a reliable witness any more."

"That bastard."

Bonnie reached for Asher's hand and encouraged him to sit with her. "We have enough evidence to take to the police. We can show them that both Galvin and Kieran are involved. Or, we can only show them one. It's up to you."

"I need to think about it, I'm sorry." Asher got up and left the room. A few seconds later, they heard the front door open and close.

Bonnie stood up, but Rez stopped her. "I'll go. I think I have more explaining to do than you. Before I do, I wonder if you'd help me with one more thing?"

"What?"

"That pocket watch in your bag? Will you help me return it to the British Museum?"

New flames ignited inside her, plans began to form in her head. The thrill of the job would always draw her in. Stealing wasn't just in her blood, it was her heartbeat.

"I'd love to."

24

"Dhruv," Bonnie said. "We need a rooftop getaway." She had no intention of using it, but the police would expect it. If they wanted to divert them, she needed to have them looking up while they snuck out the front door. "Lucy, can you research the watch, please? Give us a rough sketch of what we're looking for?"

"On it." Lucy's eyes twinkled with excitement. Bonnie saw a spark of inspiration as Lucy reached for a notepad.

"Okay. That's plan A. Now for B through Z, are you ready?"

Asher wore a deer-in-the-headlights look that, for some reason, filled her with satisfaction. It was fun to see him so far out of his comfort zone. After the way he'd punished her for keeping secrets, she enjoyed his discomfort.

"Maybe I'm getting cynical in my old age, but I think there's more to this," Dhruv said.

"Yeah, here's the thing... Galvin's safe is tricky. I mean, full out, highest level of security, every anti-cracking, anti-spoofing tech you can think of, relockers on top of relockers, too tough to drill tricky."

"So, you can't break it?" Asher asked.

"Hush, you!" Giulia chided him. "Bonnie is the safe-whisperer."

"The dual custody keys are a pain, and for any other safe, I'd say it was too difficult, but I only have to pick one lock. Galvin leaves his keys on the table during meetings." Martin had already used the photographs she'd snapped to replicate the key on his 3D printer, and Bonnie was searching hardware stores for a blank with the right keyway in the hope she could produce a metal copy. The other option would be to ask Uncle Jim to put her in contact with his friend with the jeweller's furnace. "Giuly, you can help Asher deal with the voice recognition, right?" Giulia nodded.

Having Asher in the crew was a boon, Giulia's voice replication software worked best with a voice that was close to the original. This particular father and son were already vocally similar, which increased their chances that the security system would accept the dupe.

"I still don't see the problem."

"The issue we have is that stealing the watch is only half the battle."

"What do you mean?" Asher wasn't following. As Bonnie looked around the room, she saw that he wasn't the only one.

"All we get from that is an, admittedly pricey, stolen pocket watch. What we really need is evidence on Reuter's dealings. Receipts, records."

There was one reason why Galvin would allow Kieran to hold the other key to his safe and it wasn't trust. It was mutually assured destruction. Bonnie was convinced that such a large safe wasn't just for a priceless pocket watch and the Anderson family passports. There was something else of interest in it.

A look of understanding slowly dawned on Asher's face. "If my father has evidence, it'll be in the safe."

"Bingo."

"So, what do we do?" Dhruv leaned forward expectantly.

"We need him to think we were targeting the watch so he doesn't suspect anything. We get close, without actually taking it. He'll panic, move it, then think he's in the clear. More importantly, we need to offer him another suspect. Someone it's in our interests to isolate."

"Divide and conquer," said Lucy.

"Quite. On the night, we can take our time to search the safe for evidence against Reuter without anyone knowing it. Galvin will think the safe was opened for the Coronation watch, that the thieves were interrupted by the alarm and he won't consider the other items in there. We'll build suspicion between Reuter and Anderson, start to sow some doubt and mistrust. And, we'll give Galvin a good reason to move the watch to his home safe, which is infinitely easier to open, given the opportunity."

Martin proved he'd been paying attention. "I thought the penthouse was Fort Knox, though?"

"I know how we can get an invitation." The hair on Bonnie's neck prickled —after last night at the hotel, she wasn't sure how he'd react to her plan. "Asher, you and I will be summoned there."

"How? The only time Galvin ever has employees at his home is for urgent disciplinary issues."

She arched one eyebrow. "What's the rule he's most upset about being broken?"

"He's sacked more people for breaking the inter-office relationship rule, but that wouldn't be urgent unless. Oh. Oh, I see." His cheeks flushed as it dawned on him. "That would be a big deal. It would get you fired."

"I know." From the moment she saw Galvin Anderson's name on that list from the insurance job, she knew her employment in the company would be short-lived. "Dhruv? I need the zipline to draw attention, but I want you to be home safe when it does. Is that possible?"

"I have a couple of ideas. I'll need my husband's brains and skills to do it."

"Wonderful. We'll make the police dizzy."

"While we're talking about the police, what do we do about them? It sounds like they're closing in on us. What if they're one step ahead of us this time?" Asher interjected.

"We have ways of staying ahead of the investigation. In fact, we can use this to throw a spanner into their case" Giulia assured them. "I've been putting a unique code into every trojan horse recently and suggested to my contact on the investigation that it could be a lead. In reality, it's a dead-end, but it will link Galvin's watch to the thefts of other questionable items."

"Speaking of, you need to make this one as obvious as possible. The police need to know this one is linked to the Ahmed job."

"Sure thing. What else do you need me to do?"

"The usual, switch off the CCTV cameras and disable the security system. Then, I'll need you to summon the cavalry."

"Set the alarms off?!" Giulia exclaimed.

"With you still inside? No." Asher said.

Bonnie shrugged. "Do you trust me?"

Five heads nodded begrudgingly. It was a start.

25

Fliss was following up on a lead, and she had a good feeling about it. The thieves never exited through the opposite building, according to the bank's CCTV, and the roof door was locked when they investigated it. She was sure the suspect was an employee of Anderson Hotels. Maamoud was cross-referencing a list of key-holding employees with his previous shortlist of party guests, staff and support personnel to find a link. The search had yielded a handful of Galvin's employees and their family who attended some of the events. She planned to follow up with everyone and check their alibis.

To cover all bases, Arif was also contacting insurers for more information about all the items in her files. More than once, the victim had been evasive about the thief's target. Arif wanted to work out his theory that the thieves could have hacked the insurers' records to find the items they stole. Things that the owner would be reluctant to bring to law enforcement.

Meanwhile, Arif's computer geek had identified a unique code used at several scenes. It narrowed down their search area and showed them which thefts were connected. The infiltration of Anderson Hotels used the same code. It was definitely her suspect. The woman. CCTV captured the woman in the black mask running from a fire escape at the back of the building. They were able to track her for a few streets until she was out of view. It confirmed that the first sighting was viable. It would be useful in making a case.

They were close. Closer than at any other point in the investigation. Fliss was sure of it. This was the win she badly needed, the success that would boost her career to new levels. High-profile, high society crimes got the attention of the upper levels (mainly because many of them belonged to high society) and an arrest in this case would be good for her image, and for her beleaguered taskforce.

"Ma'am," Maamoud said, ashen-faced and striding into the office without knocking. "I've just got off the phone from the director at Brache & Debar Insurance. They don't have an investigator called Carl Perez on the payroll."

She gasped and forgot to breathe out. Her head swam, she felt as though she'd lurched downwards. She'd been on a roller coaster, this was the same. Falling uncontrollably with no idea when, if, it would end.

"No. There must be some mistake." Fliss finally reasoned.

"No mistake, ma'am. They're sending over a real investigator tomorrow to review all the accounts Perez was able to access, this is a serious security breach for them, too." Arif looked terrified at how she might react.

How?

When he walked into her crime scene, he had been self-deprecatory and charming, and she fell for it. Fliss saw his ID but didn't think to verify it. Why had she been so fucking credulous?! She'd let him be an integral part of her investigation, and now nothing was as it seemed.

"The chain of evidence. Fuck!" She closed her eyes. "Everything he touched, everything he discovered is tainted. We have almost nothing."

She sat down in her chair and put her head in her hands. She would have to explain this to he bosses, then start the whole investigation from scratch.

After a late night at her desk, Fliss wandered into the car park under the police station. She was determined to make up for lost time on this investigation and, if she wanted to keep her job, she had to make progress, somehow. Lost in her thoughts, she didn't notice a dark-haired woman in a black jumpsuit and leather jacket lurking in the shadows, until she looked up to unlock her car.

"DI Stewart." The woman addressed her. "I believe you've been looking for me."

"I don't think so," she said. If they'd met, she didn't remember her.

The woman smiled and tilted her head to one side. "I don't suppose the context helps, and I don't think the image was very high quality."

"I don't..."

"Pardon me, I'm not usually dressed like this" She smoothed her clothing. "You'd recognise me in my black mask and blonde wig. I paid cash for the boots, by the way, but it was a nice try."

"You." Her eyes narrowed and she felt her hackles rise like she was a cornered animal.

"My associate tells me you're a good cop." The woman kept the car between herself and Fliss.

"Your associate?" Of course. "Rez?" Her eyes narrowed.

The woman smiled. "Don't feel bad that he fooled you, he's one of the best in the business. Look up the 1970 break-in at the British Museum if you want to see his work. He thinks you could be a great ally." Fliss scoffed. "That's why I have an offer for you."

"What makes you think I want to hear an offer from you?"

The woman smiled thinly "Because your investigation is going nowhere, and I know you want to take down some bad guys."

"You're one of the bad guys, I could take you down." Fliss knew it was an empty threat, but she had to keep up the bravado.

"If you had any proof, you'd have me in cuffs right now. I'd get out of them easily, for what it's worth. Anyway, am I really the bad guy? Worse than the people who trade in illegal items? Worse than ones who smuggle conflict diamonds? What about the people who buy those illicit objects?"

"I'd gladly arrest those people if I had any proof," Fliss said. "But you're still a thief."

The woman nodded. "I am, yes. And, Kieran Reuter, the man you questioned after the Anderson robbery is the middleman for a black-market antiquities ring. He was also, incidentally, one of the bidders on Prince Ahmed's pink diamond. I wonder who he was representing? That would be interesting."

"Why are you telling me this?" Fliss asked.

"If Reuter had a fit of conscience, or, I don't know, accidentally emailed a folder of evidence implicating himself in a number of illegal deals, that would be good news for you, I assume."

"Obviously, but how?"

The woman walked around the car towards Fliss now and handed her a business card. "My offer. You catch the bad guys and lead the investigation away from me."

It was blank except for a telephone number. "I guess this is a burner phone?"

"Completely untraceable. Call me." The woman grinned, and Fliss was disconcertingly reminded of Rez's almost cocky confidence.

"What if I'd rather catch you and your associate?" She called out.

"You can try."

A motorbike pulled up, the driver in red and black leathers. The woman took the proffered helmet and put it on. She mounted the bike, turned back to Fliss and waved. She watched them race out of the car park before getting into her car, but she didn't drive anywhere.

Turning the card over in her hands, Fliss tried to pretend she hadn't already made her decision. After ten minutes she sighed and reached for her phone. The number rang out, but as soon as she hung up, a text arrived: CHECK YOUR POCKET.

She patted herself down until she found a lump in her breast pocket. Reaching into it, she pulled out a pink gemstone. The prince's diamond.

Another text message came through: WELCOME TO THE TEAM, FLISS ;)

26

"Did you think I wouldn't notice?" Galvin asked.

Oh, shit. Asher should have seen this coming. The man hadn't invited him out for dinner since the last time he got engaged, if Galvin was buying a meal, it invariably meant bad news for Asher.

"Notice what, father?"

"That my watch went missing after you and Miss Duncan were in my home? That my safe code was reset to my wedding anniversary with your mother?"

"Oh, that." He nodded. The anniversary date was petty, but Asher didn't regret it. "I mean, I won't lie, we hoped you wouldn't notice."

"Is that all you have to say for yourself?!" Galvin's voice went up an octave in his rage. He couldn't shout, not without causing a scene in the restaurant.

"Pretty much, father. What are you going to do about it? Fire Bonnie? Too late. You could call the police and tell them that your son stole an item you don't officially own that you obtained through criminal connections? I can't see that working out well for you."

Galvin flinched, and Asher saw his hands ball into fists. He snarled. "I can't, no. I can fire you and make sure you never see a penny of your inheritance."

"By all means, fire me. I never chose this industry, it was merely expected of me."

"I..."

"Exactly." Asher leaned back in his chair and crossed his arms over his chest. "I don't want to throw stones in this particular glasshouse, but in the words of WC Fields, 'you can't con an honest man.'"

"Are you suggesting that I'm crooked?"

"It's not a suggestion. You are. We could ask the British Museum for their opinion, or maybe I can have another chat with Uncle Rami, or your ex-friend, Kieran Reuter."

"I..."

Asher had rendered him speechless. It was time to reel him in. "That friend, by the way, is being arrested as we speak. You and I both know the Reuter is the main man in your little black market enterprise, but he's going to try to take you down, if he can. Meanwhile, a number of your friends and senior management team are coming forward to admit to purchasing items they now believe to be illegal. I'd hate for them to implicate you, too."

"How do you know?"

"Oh, we've been working with the police ever since Bonnie handed back the diamond. Turns out, they'd much rather arrest the big players, especially when the little guys have so much incriminating evidence against them."

"Did Ramirez put you up to this?"

Asher laughed. "I have a mind of my own, father. If you start playing along, I can protect you."

"What do you mean, playing along?" Galvin's eyes narrowed, but his tone was even once more.

"Name names. Tell us who else was bidding for the prince's diamond, for starters."

"If I don't?"

"That's fine. My weekends are already busy with mum, though so don't expect too many visits in prison from me."

"But, you need my contacts; otherwise you wouldn't be asking."

"You're not the only rich guy in London with dodgy connections, Galvin." Asher scoffed. He stood up and dropped a USB stick on the table, next to his father's wine glass. "I'm extending you a courtesy. We extracted your name and details from Reuter's records before we handed them to the police. Right now, there's no evidence to implicate you. I have the originals. If you mess us around, DI Stewart will receive an email from your account, containing a *fascinating* ZIP file."

"Asher? Why are you saving me?"

"Someone wise once said, 'we expect our parents to be there for us. When they can't be, it hurts'. I already have one parent who can't be there for me, I don't want to make it two."

"I... I don't know what to say, Asher. Thank you."

"Don't thank me yet, you're in for a PR nightmare when news gets out that your Chief Commercial Officer has been dealing in stolen artefacts. You're going to need a good Social Media Manager to deal with the fallout. I can recommend someone if you like?"

After messing about with keys for five minutes, he finally pushed the door open and kicked his shoes into the pile. Voices carried up the stairs; laughter and shouting. The sounds of friendship. Asher stopped halfway down his descent and listened, enjoying the knowledge that the noisy group below were his friends. His family.

Fitz noticed him lurking. "Come on, my boy, we're waiting for you."

Dhruv popped the cork off a bottle of champagne as soon as Asher's feet hit the kitchen floor. Everybody cheered as some of the foam spilled over the worktop.

"What are we celebrating?" Asher asked.

"Are you kidding?" Bonnie frowned as she handed him a flute of sparkling liquid. "Fliss called, they've arrested Reuter, and he's singing like the proverbial choirboy. Prince Ahmed named the buyers in his little diamond auction and verified Kieran's part in it. He's going to need an excellent lawyer to get himself out of this mess."

Asher took a sip of champagne and Uncle Rami slapped him on the back. "Besides, we have another job to plan, and this one is going to be fun."

ABOUT THE AUTHOR

Hari Sinclair began her writing career as a food writer and columnist before moving into health and parenting. Her move into fiction was prompted by a drawer full of stories and a sarcastic Frenchman. After building a community of writers through social media, she was encouraged to publish her work. Thief by Night is her debut novel.

Join her crew for news, first looks and special offers. Head to https://harisinclair.com/stay-in-touch/[1] to sign up for her newsletter.

---

1. https://harisinclair.com/mailing-list/